Anthony McGowan is a multi-award-winning author of books for adults, teenagers and younger children. He has a lifelong obsession with the natural world, and has travelled widely to study and observe it.

Books by Anthony McGowan

Leopard Adventure

ANTHONY McGOWAN

Illustrated by Nelson Evergreen

PUFFIN

PUFFIN BOOKS

Published by the Penguin Group
Penguin Books Ltd, 80 Strand, London WC2R ORL, England
Penguin Group (USA) Inc., 375 Hudson Street, New York, New York 10014, USA
Penguin Group (Canada), 90 Eglinton Avenue East, Suite 700, Toronto, Ontario, Canada M4P 2Y3
(a division of Pearson Penguin Canada Inc.)
Penguin Ireland, 25 St Stephen's Green, Dublin 2, Ireland (a division of Penguin Books Ltd)
Penguin Group (Australia), 250 Camberwell Road, Camberwell, Victoria 3124, Australia
(a division of Pearson Australia Group Pty Ltd)
Penguin Books India Pvt Ltd, 11 Community Centre, Panchsheel Park, New Delhi – 110 017, India
Penguin Group (NZ), 67 Apollo Drive, Rosedale, Auckland 0632, New Zealand
(a division of Pearson New Zealand Ltd)
Penguin Books (South Africa) (Pty) Ltd, Block D, Rosebank Office Park, 181 Jan Smuts Avenue, Parktown
North, Gauteng 2193, South Africa

Penguin Books Ltd, Registered Offices: 80 Strand, London WC2R ORL, England

puffinbooks.com

First published 2012
001 – 10 9 8 7 6 5 4 3 2 1

Text and illustrations copyright © Willard Price Literary Management Ltd, 2012
Map copyright © Puffin Books, 2012
Illustrations by Nelson Evergreen
All rights reserved

The moral right of the author and illustrator has been asserted

Set in Baskerville MT Std 13 / 16pt by Palimpsest Book Production Ltd, Falkirk, Stirlingshire
Printed in Great Britain by Clays Ltd, St Ives plc

British Library Cataloguing in Publication Data
A CIP catalogue record for this book is available from the British Library

ISBN: 978-0-141-33945-0

www.greenpenguin.co.uk

MIX
Paper from
responsible sources
FSC® C018179
www.fsc.org

Penguin Books is committed to a sustainable
future for our business, our readers and our planet.
This book is made from Forest Stewardship
Council™ certified paper.

ALWAYS LEARNING   **PEARSON**

*This book is dedicated
to the great Willard Price himself,
adventurer and storyteller*

Contents

Siberia

Vladivostok

Long Island, USA

A Big Beast in a Bad Mood

The giant forest hog was a quarter of a tonne of angry pig you really wouldn't want to mess with. Two great tusks curved up from its top jaw, and two more jutted out from the bottom. A giant forest hog in a good mood could be a dangerous beast. In a bad mood it was lethal: those tusks could open up and empty out a human stomach like a tin of beans.

And this giant forest hog was in a very bad mood. Its little piggy eyes were staring short-sightedly at Amazon Hunt. It snorted twice with a noise like a backfiring car, and then it charged.

What on earth am I doing here? thought Amazon, not for the first time over the past few days. She was a long way from home, and her only chance of survival lay in the hands of her thirteen-year-old cousin who, quite frankly, couldn't shoot to save his own life, never mind hers.

2

The Climb

Amazon's adventure had begun three days earlier and thousands of miles away.

She was craning her neck to look up at her open bedroom window, on the third floor of the dormitory block of Millbank Abbey, an English boarding school deep in the Sussex countryside. *A tough climb*, she thought, *but not impossible.*

Unless, of course, you had a secret fear of heights.

Amazon had missed her curfew again. She had been in the woods next to the school grounds, watching a family of badgers playing outside their sett. She was so engrossed in the way the little ones had fought and rolled in the dry leaves that she had completely lost track of time. She'd thought about making a dash for it through the ornate front door of the school, but if she were caught again it would be the end. The headmistress, that sour-faced old dragon, Miss Pettifer, had said that one more 'episode', and she would be confined to the creepy old building for the whole summer, and that she really couldn't bear. An 'episode' could be anything from wearing a skirt that was too short to blowing up half the chemistry lab, even though that had been an accident. Sort of . . .

It was bad enough that she was the only girl spending the summer holidays at Millbank. She'd had to wave off all her friends as they were collected by their parents, and then go back alone to the empty, echoing dorm. Sometimes she wished her parents' lives were a bit less . . . interesting, then hers might not be quite so boring.

So she started to climb. The first part was easy enough – there was an old iron drainpipe attached to the wall by thick brackets, which made excellent hand and footholds for her strong fingers and nimble feet. Soon she was up to the first-floor level.

Then she looked down.

Mistake.

Instantly her head began to spin. She thought for a moment that she might actually puke, which added a whole layer of grossness on top of the wobbling jelly of her fear, making the world's nastiest trifle. She breathed deeply, swallowed hard and got a grip on her insides before reaching for the next hold. A minute later she reached the second floor. Her arms were beginning to ache, so she took a rest. This time she didn't look down. But she did wonder what would happen if she fell.

Sprained ankle?

Broken leg?

Broken neck?

She knew that this was reckless, but also that it would now be just as difficult to climb back down as to go on. Hadn't she read somewhere that most mountaineering accidents happen when the climbers are on the way down?

She gulped, and climbed again. She was there, so nearly there. The open window called to her in a sweet, soft voice. But it was now that the fatal flaw in her plan became evident: somehow she had to get from the drainpipe to the window ledge.

She stretched out her hand. She could just touch the corner of the ledge with her fingertips. It wasn't enough. She was going to have to jump. She thought again about the drop; about the horror as she fell through the air; about the agonizing crunch at the bottom.

But Amazon, despite her phobia, was no coward. She tensed her muscles and leapt sideways across the face of the wall.

It was a good jump.

She was going to make it.

Her fingers found the window ledge, and gripped. But the plaster was old and crumbly. To Amazon's dismay she found that her fingers were slipping. She scrabbled vainly at the ledge. She was falling. She tried to dig her nails into the very wall itself, but it was no good. It flaked away and took her hopes with it.

She thought, briefly, about screaming. But she wasn't a screaming sort of a girl.

Her final thoughts were of her mum and dad, how she wished that she could see them again, one last time . . .

3

New Friends

And then came a jolt as a hand closed round her wrist. She gasped in amazement, and looked up. Leaning out of the window was a kid with messy, floppy hair. His grey eyes looked vaguely familiar, although she was sure she'd never met him before.

'Hi, cuz,' he said. 'Call me old-fashioned, but I always say you can't beat the door for, you know, getting in and out of a room.'

The boy tugged, and Amazon somehow found a toehold in the ancient brickwork. As soon as she got her knees up on to the window ledge, Amazon shook off the kid's hand.

'Who the heck are you?' she said in a voice that wasn't far short of a snarl.

'Hey, Amazon by name, Amazon by nature,' said the kid, still grinning.

'What are you talking about?' she snapped.

'Just saying, you know, cool Greek girl warriors . . . you climbing up the wall like Spider-Man, an' all.'

'I know who the flaming Amazons were. But you still haven't told me who you are.'

The grin grew even wider. 'I'm your cousin, Frazer Hunt. And I think that maybe I just saved your neck. If I hadn't looked out –'

'I was fine. I'd have made it,' lied Amazon. She knew that she had a cousin called Frazer, though she'd never met him. Just then she noticed another figure standing in the shadows. 'Who's this guy?'

The figure stepped forward. He was tall, but stooping, wore rimless glasses and was almost completely bald. He held out his hand.

'Doctor John Drexler. Pleased to meet you.'

Amazon didn't take the hand. She was still suspicious. She'd been taken by surprise, and that was one thing she didn't like.

'What's this all about?'

'I think I'd rather explain when we're safely airborne,' said Dr Drexler. 'And we really must hurry if we're to make that flight.'

'Airborne? Flight? What is this? Where are we going?'

'Well, to New York and then the TRACKS base on Long Island. Your uncle, Hal, awaits, and your mother and father should have arrived by the time we get there.'

'Mum and Dad? What are they doing there? And I can't just leave . . . Miss Pettifer – she'll never allow it.'

7

'On the contrary,' came a sharp voice, and Amazon spun round to see the equally sharp face of Miss Pettifer, who had bustled into the now rather crowded room. 'I have received an email from your parents. You are to leave with these people.'

Miss Pettifer didn't try to hide her distaste. In fact, as Amazon guessed, she was torn between relief at getting rid of Amazon (whose fees had already been paid, without the option of a refund), and her annoyance that it should occur in such an unusual way.

'Can I see the email?' Amazon asked.

'Of course,' replied Miss Pettifer frostily. 'Here is a printout.'

She handed Amazon an A4 sheet of paper. The message was in two parts. The first was addressed to Miss Pettifer from Amazon's mother, Ling-Mei, and simply informed her that Amazon would not be staying for the summer. The second part was addressed to Amazon.

It read:

Darling Amazon,

Your father and I have had to cut short our expedition to Alaska. We have come across some very important information, and need to discuss the issue with your uncle, Hal. We think it best if you come to meet us at the old ranch on Long Island where your father was brought up, and from where Hal now runs his animal rescue organization. Hal is sending one of his assistants,

Dr Drexler, along with his son, your cousin Frazer, to collect
you. I don't want to sound too mysterious, but I really can't tell
you any more about this until we meet you on Long Island.

   Lots of love,

   Mum (and Dad says don't eat too many olives on the plane!)

That certainly rang true. Amazon's strangely adult taste for black olives was a standing joke in the family.

She looked again at the people in the room. Frazer had a face it was hard not to like, even if you were naturally a little suspicious of people, as was Amazon. Dr Drexler was trickier to read, but he seemed harmless enough. And then there was Miss Pettifer with her cat's-bum mouth. That, at least, was one very good reason to get out of this place.

But even more than the joy of escaping from Miss Pettifer, Amazon was excited about seeing her mum and dad. They had been away on some mysterious expedition for four months, and in all that time she had only had one hurried phone call, cut short when the satellite link had gone down. And secretly she was excited about what, in her heart of hearts, she knew was going to be an adventure.

'Just give me five minutes to pack,' she said.

At this same moment, five thousand miles away, a mother Amur leopard, one of the rarest big cats in the world, was sniffing the air suspiciously.

It should have been a good time. The two cubs had fed on her rich milk, and they now wormed their way cosily into her thick fur.

But she was worried. There were only two animals she feared. The first were humans with their killing sticks that made the noise of thunder. The second was the tiger. Humans had been in the woods with dogs. And she had smelled the strong odour of a big male tiger two days ago.

But something else was coming, something that was faster than any human, more deadly than a tiger. Something that would find her even in the deepest den.

Again she sniffed. A memory stirred. Carefully, she picked up both of her cubs. They mewled and complained in their sleepy way. She ignored their cries and prowled away silently through the thick undergrowth.

She could not have known that as she was moving away from her fear, she was walking right into a trap.

4
Amazon Tastes the High Life

Three hours later, Amazon was sitting in the luxury of first class, with her cousin Frazer on one side and Dr Drexler on the other. They were 35,000 feet above the Atlantic.

Her parents didn't have much money to spare. Almost every penny left over from their environmental work went on her boarding-school fees, so this was the first time she had flown in anything other than the cheapest seats. She felt like a princess sitting on a throne. And they had *four different kinds of olives*, which they'd bring you whenever you asked!

But despite the comfort and luxury – or maybe even *because* of them – she was still troubled and confused. Something about this just didn't make sense to Amazon. Her father, Roger Hunt, had fallen out with his brother, Hal, years before. As far as she knew, they hadn't spoken a word since she was a baby. What could be so important that they had arranged this family reunion?

If only her parents had written more in that email . . .

She looked over at Frazer. He was eating pretzels and playing with his new toy: a cool little Leica digital camera that cost so much you'd think it was made of solid gold. She was beginning to like him, but she didn't think he was the one to answer her questions. She turned to Dr Drexler, who was reading a magazine called *The Journal of Veterinary Science*.

'So let me get this straight,' she said. 'My mum and dad are definitely waiting for me on Long Island?'

Dr Drexler put down the magazine, and looked at her over the top of his reading glasses.

'That is my, *ah*, expectation. They sent a message, letting your uncle Hal know that they had something of vital importance to tell him. They added that you should be brought over to the TRACKS HQ as well. But they had not yet arrived when Frazer and I set off.'

Dr Drexler said 'ah' quite a lot, as if he were always searching for exactly the right word. It fitted in with his general fussy appearance. He had the cleanest nails Amazon had ever seen.

'Why didn't they just come and get me?'

'It wasn't possible. They were flying in directly from . . . well, I'm not quite sure which far-flung part of the world . . .' Dr Drexler chuckled a little nervously, or so Amazon thought. He took a sip of the dry martini that had been served to him by an elegant, smiling stewardess. 'Tell me, Amazon, what do you know about Hal Hunt's organization?'

'We're called TRACKS,' cut in Frazer. 'I helped come up with the name. It stands for . . . hold on, let me get this right, the Trans-Regional Animal Conservation and Knowledge Society. I know it's a bit of a mouthful, but all the really snappy names had already been taken, and there were copyright issues to think about. Anyway, like I said, we just call it TRACKS, and we are the Trackers. Pretty cool, huh?'

Amazon made a non-committal *hummmph* noise. 'I've heard my parents talking about it. They say it's a big organization *supposedly* set up to help animals, but –'

'Supposedly?'

'Yeah, well, my dad says that you take money from millionaires and big business, and *they* sure don't have a good record for caring about the environment. My dad says that Uncle Hal sold out, that he abandoned all his old ideals. And,' she added, looking rather guiltily at her olive, 'I dread to think what he'd say about flying first class like this. I mean, shouldn't the money be spent on something more . . . important?'

'That's not fair!' exclaimed Frazer. 'This airline is one of our corporate sponsors, so we get the flights for nothing. Dad couldn't do all the cool stuff he does without the money he drags in.'

Dr Drexler patted the boy's arm. 'That's OK, Frazer. Amazon doesn't know the truth about us yet. She'll come to appreciate our work when she gets to know us a little better.' He turned back to Amazon. 'Let me try to give you a more, ah, *realistic* picture of our organization and what we do. As I'm sure you know, Hal Hunt is one of the most respected conservationists and animal experts in the world. He set up what was to become TRACKS with your father, Roger, twenty years ago.'

'Yeah, sure, but my dad walked out because of all the interference from the guys in suits.'

'As you say,' Dr Drexler carried on patiently, 'your father left the organization at an early stage. There were differences about the way we should do things, but no real argument about the underlying purpose. TRACKS is dedicated to providing state-of-the-art training and resources to young conservationists. The, ah, Trackers act as a flying squad, ready to take off at a moment's notice to rescue wild animals in danger wherever they may be. Of course most of the team are over eighteen, but Frazer here has already helped out on a couple of missions. That right, ah, Fraze?'

Frazer blushed, but still looked pretty pleased. 'Yeah, I guess, sorta. Cos of my dad. Mainly I just take photos, you know, recording the work.' He held up the camera for Amazon to admire. 'Got this baby to help me out when I didn't want to carry anything bigger.'

'As well as these field missions,' Dr Drexler continued, 'TRACKS also runs captive-breeding programmes to support conservation projects. Recently, for example, we've been involved in returning red pandas to the foothills of the Himalayas. And, finally, we provide equipment and resources to other wildlife charities and organizations. We really are the good guys, you know. And there's always room for eager new recruits . . .'

Amazon was taken aback. Was Drexler asking her to become a Tracker?

'What, you mean . . .?'

'All things are possible. We can discuss it with your parents, when we see them.'

'And what exactly do you do in all this, apart from babysit Frazer?' asked Amazon, her doubts still adding a hard edge to her voice.

Dr Drexler twitched, and there was a cold twinkle behind his spectacles as he replied, 'I'm TRACKS's chief veterinary surgeon.'

'He's good,' said Frazer. 'Look, he even cut out my appendix when we were in Mozambique and I couldn't get to the hospital. He used a penknife and, well, I don't know, a spoon or something.'

Frazer pulled up his shirt, to show a neat purple scar.

Amazon rolled her eyes.

'You exaggerate somewhat, Frazer,' said Dr Drexler. 'I had a proper medical kit. But thank you, anyway. And can I now suggest that we all take this opportunity to get a little rest. Tomorrow will be a busy day.'

Their first-class seats converted into beds. Soon the lights dimmed, and in a few minutes Amazon heard gentle snores coming from one side, and a low mumbling, as of someone talking in their sleep, from the other.

There were so many things on her mind, so many unanswered questions that she thought she would never sleep, but eventually she drifted into unconsciousness and found herself lost in a dream of hot pursuit and fear, and of a snarling mouth full of glistening teeth.

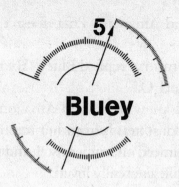

5

Bluey

They were met at JFK Airport by a tall, young, suntanned Australian guy.

'Hey, Zonnie,' he said, inventing Amazon's new nickname on the spot. 'I'm Bluey.' He pointed at his mop of violently red hair, as if that explained everything.

Frazer winked at her. 'Zonnie – that's gonna stick!' She gave him a playful slap – the first of what would turn out to be many.

Bluey showed them to a big, growling jeep that took up two spaces in the parking lot.

'Not very environmentally friendly,' said Amazon as they climbed into the air-conditioned interior. Her own parents drove an electric car whenever they were back in England.

'This old girl?' said Bluey. 'Nah – she's been adapted to run on hydrogen. The only emission she gives off is pure water.'

'Really?' said Amazon. 'That doesn't seem very likely.'

'Simple chemistry,' replied Bluey. 'Hydrogen plus oxygen equals H_2O.'

'Hummff, I knew that,' said Amazon, annoyed that she had forgotten it from her science lessons. She'd always drifted off in chemistry and physics – it was biology that she really loved.

It took three hours to drive to the TRACKS HQ, first along the highway, then on smaller roads and finally down bumpy country tracks.

Bluey and Frazer chatted away about the Trackers, and Frazer got very excited when Bluey told him that something called the 'X-Ark', whatever that might be, had arrived. Their enthusiasm was infectious, and Amazon found herself smiling, almost against her will, at the stories of polar bear cubs and dolphins and wallabies. Her parents had never taken her on any of their expeditions, and she was suddenly jealous of the lives of Frazer and his friends.

Could it really be true that she might become one of them?

Making TRACKS

The old farm that had become the TRACKS HQ was half hidden in the folds of a green valley, a couple of miles from the sea. After all the talk of technology and investment, Amazon had expected gleaming metal and glass, like something from a sci-fi movie. However, the scene before her now was charmingly rustic. There was a large, old farmhouse with a porch, two huge barns, a stable block, fields and paddocks. The only thing that marked it out from any other American farm was the variety of animals grazing in the fields.

Amazon felt instantly excited, and it wasn't just the prospect of seeing her parents. Her mouth fell open as she spotted a couple of zebras, a small herd of wildebeest, a mother rhino with her calf, and a bizarre-looking bird like a small, grumpy ostrich with a blue neck and a vicious-looking bony crest on the top of its head.

'That's Lady Gaga, our cassowary,' said Bluey,

noticing the direction of her gaze. 'Watch out for her – if she doesn't headbutt you, she'll give you a good old slash with those claws. Nearest thing around here to a velociraptor.'

They pulled up outside the farmhouse, and a young woman wearing a white lab coat came out to meet them. She strode forward, looking very serious. Amazon got the impression that even if there were nothing serious for her to look serious about, she'd still look serious. She had serious glasses and serious hair and a very serious nose. Without saying anything to the others, she took Dr Drexler to one side and whispered in his ear.

He turned back, and Amazon knew at once that something was wrong.

'Let me introduce you to Miranda Coverdale, my veterinary assistant.'

The woman nodded curtly, and Dr Drexler continued. 'It would seem that there's been a change of plan. I'm afraid that your parents, Amazon, haven't managed to make it here, quite, *ah*, yet. And it also appears that your father, Frazer, has gone off to . . . well, er, for want of a better word, find them.'

Amazon felt a little wave of fear pass through her. She shook it off, the way you'd shrug away a whining mosquito.

'They're always getting lost. It's what they do,' she said, trying to be brave.

'Wherever they are, my dad will find them. It's

what *he* does.' Frazer smiled at Amazon, and for the first time she smiled back. 'Let me show you up to your room,' he said. 'It's next door to mine.'

Together they walked to the farmhouse. On the ground floor there was a big kitchen, a living room and a library full of old books. Amazon's room was up in the attic. It was small and rather bare, but comfortable enough after the horrors of Millbank Abbey.

'You get settled in. After lunch I'll show you round the place,' said Frazer. 'You'll like it here, honest. And I know your parents will be fine. Dad'll bring them back.'

Amazon nodded, but said nothing.

Lunch was sandwiches in the kitchen, eaten with half a dozen other Trackers. Frazer introduced them all, but it was too much for Amazon to take in, and they blended together into one big bundle of youth and enthusiasm and excited talk of animals and rainforests and oceans.

7

The Grand Tour

After lunch, Frazer and Bluey gave Amazon what they called 'the grand tour'.

'Everything here's powered by solar energy,' Frazer gushed, apparently hoping this would impress his cousin.

'And when it rains?'

'We have a mini-hydro plant that acts as a backup.' Luckily, Frazer had a lot of patience, with both animals and people.

They began the tour with the barns, which were divided up into sections containing all kinds of smaller animals. There were cages with tiny marmosets – golden-haired primates no bigger than kittens. Bluey opened a cage and let Amazon feed them pieces of cut-up apple as they perched on the palm of her hand.

Other cages contained cold-eyed lizards as long as Amazon's arm.

'What are they?' she asked.

'Komodo dragons. Babies. When they grow up they'll be big enough to take down a buffalo. They have venomous saliva that rots your flesh.'

Amazon decided against having a go at feeding the dragons.

There was a big outdoor aviary full of noisy parrots, toucans with huge colourful beaks and ominous fruit bats hanging upside down wrapped in their leathery wings. Then they came to an enclosure with a pool, in which wallowed a pair of pigmy hippos.

'There're only a few hundred left in the wild,' said Frazer.

One of the hippos waddled over. It came up to Amazon's waist.

'Sweet,' said Amazon. She put her arm through the fence, meaning to stroke the dark grey nose.

Then she remembered something her father had told her: a full-sized hippo, despite its almost comical appearance, was just about the most dangerous animal in Africa. It could bite a person clean in half with one crunch of its huge jaws. This guy was only a quarter of the size of its bigger relative, but still . . . She pulled her arm back in the nick of time – the pygmy hippo snapped at her with vicious ten-centimetre-long canines.

The little tyrant snorted dismissively, and waddled off again, having shown the world who was boss.

'You OK?' said Frazer anxiously.

Amazon laughed with relief at her narrow escape.

'Yeah, sure, just about. That ga-ga cassowary, the dragon, the hippo . . . Is there anything here that doesn't want to kill me?'

'I know something,' said Frazer, 'come with me.'

Leaving Bluey with the hippos Frazer led the way to the stables. 'Can you ride?' he asked.

There was genuine longing in Amazon's voice as she replied. 'I'm not very good, but I can, sort of. I've always loved horses, and my dad always promised me a pony, but we never lived anywhere long enough or big enough to get one. But I had some lessons last summer.'

As they approached, a long grey head appeared over one of the stalls.

'Hey, look, there's Joey. He's my horse.' Frazer went over and took the soft muzzle in his hands breathing gently into the horse's nose.

'He's beautiful,' sighed Amazon.

'He is. And kind too. Not a mean bone in his body. We can ride out tomorrow if you like – there's a lot more to see.'

'I'd love that.'

'You can have Joey, and I'll take Sheba – she's more of a handful.'

On cue, a black head joined the grey one, and blew a loud raspberry, spraying Amazon with slobber.

'Eeew!' she squealed, but there was laughter in her voice.

*

That night Amazon lay awake a long time thinking about everything that had happened to her. It was only a little over a day ago that she was stuck in Millbank Abbey, with nothing but her badgers to look forward to. And now here she was on the other side of the Atlantic, surrounded by zebras.

Zebras!

And then there was Frazer. He wasn't dumb, by any means, but he had a kind of simplicity and openness that made it impossible not to like him.

And yet there was the nagging fear about her mum and dad. If only they were here everything would be perfect.

She got up and padded over to the chest of drawers into which she'd dumped her clothes. In the bottom drawer she found what she was looking for: a red neckerchief with white spots, faded and worn smooth with time. It had been a present to her mum from her dad on their first expedition together, years and years ago. And then her mother had given it to Amazon before she'd gone on the latest trip.

She climbed back into bed, wrapped the neckerchief round her fingers and breathed through the old material. Although it was clean and fresh, the neckerchief still somehow smelled both of her mother and of the exciting places she had visited: Africa, the Himalayas, dark jungles and scorched deserts.

As she drifted towards sleep, Amazon remembered one of the few times that they had all been able to spend the whole summer together. They'd gone sailing in the Lake District. It was the happiest time of her life. And soon she was dreaming of light sparkling on water, and the tinkling sound of her mother's sweet laughter, and the kind touch of her father's hands as he taught her how to tie knots and whittle sticks.

8

Frazer's New Toy

The next morning there was still no sign of either Amazon's parents or Frazer's father.

'No word yet,' said Dr Drexler, smiling sympathetically.

Amazon thought she detected something uncertain behind the smile. It wasn't quite as if he were trying to hide something he knew – more, she thought, that he was trying to convince himself that everything was OK.

Frazer noticed it too. Frazer's response to any troubling news or awkward situation was always the same: throw yourself into action.

'Come on,' he said enthusiastically. 'Let's go for that ride, before it gets too hot.'

'That's a fine idea,' said Dr Drexler. 'You could ride out to the enclosure with the giant forest hogs. I'm going over that way with Miranda to take a look at the old boar. I think he's got a bad tooth and I may have to extract it. You can use your new toy to put him under, Frazer.'

'My X-Ark! Awesome idea!' agreed Frazer.

The X-Ark turned out to be a very hi-tech tranquillizer gun, moulded from a gleaming metal alloy. Amazon hated guns, but even she thought it looked pretty cool, in a Star Warsy kind of way.

'Remember when you missed that elephant in Namibia, Fraze? From, what was it . . . four metres?' chuckled Bluey. 'You could have reached out and poked the dart right in him.' Turning to Amazon he added, 'Poor old Frazer here can shoot anything with his camera, but put a tranq gun in his hands and he's completely –'

'That wasn't my fault! I was in a tree, and it was windy. And the sights were bent on my last rifle. But the X-Ark comes with a laser scope. Can't miss.'

'We'll see,' said Dr Drexler. 'Even more importantly, it's a chance to field-test the new tranquillizer mix we've developed for the darts. We put a lot of time and money into researching it, Amazon. As well as an unusually fast-acting anaesthetic, it contains a paralysing agent extracted from the skin glands of certain South American tree frogs, which takes effect almost instantaneously. Normally, when you dart an animal, it can take several minutes to go under, and that can be dangerous – for you and the animal. But the new mix just turns the lights right out. That, at least, is the theory, and so far the laboratory tests have corroborated it.'

Amazon shrugged. It was all quite interesting, but didn't seem particularly relevant to her.

'Bluey,' Dr Drexler continued, 'perhaps you could drive Miranda and me out to the giant forest hogs in the jeep. We'll meet you two over there.'

Amazon and Frazer walked through the morning mist to the stables. Frazer helped Amazon get Joey saddled. She had forgotten the sheer fun of just being around horses: the rich smell, the snuffly sounds they made when they were happy, the sudden exhilarating moment when they startled and you realized how immensely powerful they were. It was all exactly what Amazon needed to take her mind off her parents.

She'd grabbed a couple of sugar lumps from the breakfast table, and soon Joey was her best friend. He'd slobbered all over her hand as she fed him, and then blew a raspberry in her ear.

'It's his way of saying that he likes you,' laughed Frazer as she cleaned out her ear with a handkerchief. 'Here, you'd better take this,' he said, handing her a hard riding hat. Joey's as gentle as a kitten, but if you're not used to riding –'

She shook her head. 'No way! I'm in America; I'm on a ranch – I want one of those!' She pointed to a Stetson hanging from a peg.

'This is not a ranch and —'

'Just gimme the flaming cowboy hat!'

It was pointless arguing with his English cousin, and as this particular Stetson had a built-in helmet Frazer could appear to let Amazon win this one, and save it up as credit. He gave her the hat.

'How do I look?' she said, striking a pose.

'Like a rootin' tootin' cowgirl.'

'Oh. Are rootin' and tootin' good things?'

'I have no idea. Now shall we get on? I have an enormous pig to shoot.'

Luckily there was a mounting block to help the riders climb into the saddle. Frazer held Joey's reins while Amazon climbed on board, and then adjusted her stirrups.

Once she was safely in the saddle, Amazon realized something: she'd never been on a horse this big before. She felt as though she were a hundred metres off the ground. Easily high enough, in fact, for her fear of heights to kick in. She pulled her mother's neckerchief from her pocket and tied it round her neck for luck.

'You OK, Zonnie?' Frazer asked. He had already swung himself effortlessly into the saddle, like he was just throwing on a jacket.

Amazon gulped. She really wanted to climb down again, but she wasn't going to let Frazer see that she was afraid. She forced herself to smile, and gave a jaunty thumbs-up sign.

'Just follow me, then,' said Frazer, and he led the frisky Sheba down the track.

Amazon dug her heels into Joey. Nothing happened for a second or two, then the horse looked round at her, blew one of his famous raspberries and followed Sheba.

9

Cowgirl Amazon

Soon they were trotting through the gently rolling countryside. The sky above them was so clear and blue Amazon found it hard to believe that it could ever be cloudy again. Joey was placid and easy to ride, and her fear had burned away like the morning mist.

'Looking good, Zonnie. Can you gallop?' asked Frazer.

'Yes. Er, no. Maybe. Let's try!'

Amazon had only galloped once before, on a little show pony, but she was learning fast. Joey seemed to know what she wanted before she had fully formed the thought.

Frazer led them down a shortcut through the field with the zebra and wildebeest, and urged Sheba into a canter. Amazon followed, nervous at first as Joey picked up speed, but gaining confidence as he moved into an exhilarating gallop. The African animals scattered at the sight of the galloping horses, the wildebeest honking like angry geese, and the zebra whinnying and bucking. Sheba whinnied back, and Frazer had to fight hard to control her, but Joey was as smooth and relaxed as melted butter.

'This is the best fun I've ever had in my entire life,' yelled Amazon, her voice carrying away like a banner in the wind behind her.

In twenty minutes they'd reached the enclosure: a slice of primordial swamp, dumped down on Long Island. There was a sty at the far end, and as she slowed Joey back to a trot Amazon could hear contented pig noises, mingled with deeper grunts and a few high-pitched squeals.

They pulled the horses to a halt next to the fence that surrounded the enclosure. Amazon took off the hat and untied the neckerchief to wipe the sweat from her brow.

'Piglets in there,' said Frazer, 'so we have to be . . .' He was going to say 'careful', but just then a gust of wind came out of nowhere. It blew Amazon's neckerchief from her grasp, then it sailed over the fence and landed in the mud.

Amazon wailed in despair at losing her precious keepsake. Without thinking, she stood up in the stirrups, pulled out one foot and swung her leg across Joey's back. In one fluid movement, she jumped over the fence and into the soft mud of the enclosure after the neckerchief. She sprawled forward, her face slithering through the pungent, green-tinged slime.

Frazer's desperate cry of 'NOOOOOOOOOO!' was too late for Amazon.

10

A Sticky Situation

Frazer had watched with surprise, admiration and then horror as Amazon jumped into the enclosure.

His 'Noooooooo!' was the classic warning to 'duck' after you've already been punched. He had failed to tell Amazon two crucial facts.

The first was that the giant forest hog is ferocious and mean – maybe not quite up there with the hippo, but definitely not to be taken lightly.

The second was an important thing about the fence.

Amazon pulled herself up out of what she sincerely hoped was only mud with a great, wet sucking noise, and struggled towards her neckerchief, which had blown right into the middle of the pen.

'The fence, Zonnie,' Frazer yelled. 'Don't touch it!'

Amazon turned back towards Frazer.

'What?'

'It's electrified. You won't be able to climb out.'

'Oh. Where's the gate?'

Frazer pointed down to the other end of the enclosure, near the sty.

And at that moment the giant forest hog boar appeared, looking, to Amazon, as big as the horse she'd just jumped off. It was, undoubtedly, the ugliest animal she had ever seen. It was covered in straggly black hair, which showed the flabby reddish skin of its great sagging belly beneath. Its scarred and knobbly face, along with the tusks, made it look more like a mythological monster than a real creature.

And those tusks – brown and rotten-looking, but still lethal – were designed to grind against each other to sharpen their cutting edge.

Amazon might not always get on well with people, but she'd made friends with every animal she'd ever met. However, she felt instinctively that this beast was never going to be her friend.

She was right.

The boar had toothache. He also had a job. That job was defending the piglets, which were squirming over and under and all around Mrs Giant Hog. These two ideas came fuzzily together in his mind. He saw Amazon and he perceived a threat. And something deep in his brain thought that having a good old gore might just help that sore tooth of his.

Amazon looked round again at Frazer.

He'd disappeared. She didn't know what to do.

The only way out was past the enormous boar.

Who was staring . . .
Who was grunting . . .
Who was snorting . . .
Who was charging . . .!

11

Frazer's Shot

Amazon couldn't see Frazer because he had jumped down from his horse and run to the jeep, which was just pulling up – Bluey behind the wheel.

'No time to explain,' cried Frazer to the startled Australian as he pulled open the tailgate of the jeep.

With fumbling fingers, he flicked the catches on the metal case and took out the coldly gleaming X-Ark. Luckily, there was already a dart in the chamber.

He reached the fence just as the boar began its charge. He had three seconds at the most. His hands were sweating, and more sweat poured down his face and into his eyes.

He aimed, looking for the red dot of the laser sight.

It was no good. Amazon was in the way. There was no time for him to move sideways.

Only one chance.

He threw himself down on to the floor, and aimed

through the fence and between Amazon's legs. Yes! He had a shot. He took a deep breath to steady himself, the way his dad had taught him. And then, aiming for the rippling muscle on the boar's mighty shoulder, he gently squeezed the trigger, being careful not to jerk or pull.

The tranquillizer gun was powered by a small canister of compressed carbon dioxide gas. There was barely a sound as the dart flew from the barrel, and – unlike with a hunting rifle – only the tiniest of kicks.

Yes, this was a good gun, thought Frazer, his mind working at the speed of light.

And this was a good shot. It was said that a great marksman always knew when a shot went home, even with their eyes closed, just by the feel of it. All Bluey's jokes would bounce off him now. He was the hero. He had saved Amazon. His dad would be so proud.

And then he heard the small, but distinct *thock* as the tranquillizer dart hit flesh.

Not, alas, the bristling hairy hide covering the giant forest hog's shoulder, but the denim covering Amazon Hunt's left butt-cheek.

Amazon had time only to register the sharp impact, half turn towards Frazer, a look of puzzlement on her face, before her eyes rolled up into her head and she pitched back down into the mud, right under the thundering feet of the giant forest hog.

12

The Mission

'It was all part of my brilliant plan,' grinned Frazer.

It was the following morning and Frazer, Bluey and Miranda Coverdale were standing around Amazon's bed. Amazon had a thumping headache and a major pain in her butt, but she found it hard not to smile at her cousin's performance.

'Look,' Frazer went on. 'You're a little slimmer than a giant forest hog, right?'

'Gee, thanks. And you're a little smarter than a brain-damaged donkey.'

'Oh, OK, cool. You're still upset – I get that. I shot you in the . . . Anyway, I knew that it would take longer for the tranquillizer to work on that great fat pig than it would on you. If I'd hit the hog, it would still have time to mess you up good with those tusks. But if I darted *you* then you'd be down and out in a blink, and the hog would realize that you were no threat. And that's what happened. As soon as it knew

42

its ugly little piglets were safe, it waddled off back to its sty. It was sheer genius, really.'

Amazon looked round at the others. 'Ha! The new tranquillizer mix could have taken down the hog instantly, and you know it! Does anyone actually believe my idiot cousin?'

Bluey grinned. 'She's right, Fraze – plus you couldn't hit the barn, never mind the barn door.'

'Could so hit the barn door! I've been practising. But who cares? Whether or not I meant it, it all worked out for the best, didn't it? I reckon I saved your, er, butt out there!'

Then Amazon remembered something. 'My neckerchief!'

'That old thing,' said Frazer innocently. 'I gave it to the hog. He looks kind of cute with it tied round his tail.'

And then, before Amazon could whack him, he pulled it out of his pocket.

'Got it washed and ironed for you.' He grinned. 'I guessed it meant something . . . you know, important.'

'Thanks,' said Amazon, and gave her cousin a grateful smile.

At that moment Dr Drexler appeared. He looked even greyer and more worried than usual. Amazon assumed it was because he was worried about her. He was in charge of this TRACKS place while her uncle Hal was away and so he'd be held responsible if anything went wrong. And Amazon getting shot

– even if it was only with a tranquillizer dart – counted as something going wrong.

'Feeling, *ah*, better are we this morning?'

'Head hurts. And my bu– er . . . yeah . . . not too bad.'

'Well, that's good, because we may need a little help with something.'

'A mission?' Frazer cut in, almost yelling with excitement.

'That's right.'

'What's the job?' asked Bluey, sounding almost as excited as Frazer.

'It's in the Sikhote-Alin mountain range in the Primorsky Krai region.'

'The *what*?' asked a puzzled Amazon. 'In the *where*?' She was pretty good at geography, but she'd never heard of those mountains or that region.

'It's the far east of Russia, bordered to the south by Korea, in the west by China, and to the east by the Sea of Japan.'

'Tigers,' said Frazer. 'It's got to be Siberian tigers, right? I totally love saving stuff that really wants to, like, *eat* me.'

Amazon glanced over at Frazer. She'd assumed that he was joking, but it looked like he actually meant it.

'You are one weird kid,' she said, shaking her head.

'Not tigers this time, Frazer,' said Dr Drexler. 'It's

something even more endangered than Siberian tigers. It's the Amur leopard – the rarest big cat in the world. We've been helping to fund a reintroduction programme in the north of the leopard's old range. We've been contacted by our link man out there, an American scientist, who's part of the local conservation effort. He tells me that at least one of the leopards has been cut off by a forest fire. He hasn't got the resources to deal with the situation, and so we're sending in a team to try to rescue the animal.'

Frazer didn't look *too* disappointed. 'Hey, leopards are pretty cool. There was a famous one in India that ate three hundred people. I read about it in a book.'

'You've read a book?' said Amazon sweetly. 'With words in? Or was it just pictures? Maybe you coloured it in with your crayons.'

But Frazer was too buoyed up to be annoyed. It took more than a bit of sarcasm to ruin his mood when an expedition was in the air.

'I'll let that one ride,' he said, 'seeing as I just shot you in the butt and all. But keep it up and I'll tranquillize your other cheek . . .'

'Aim for her butt next time and you'll definitely hit the hog,' laughed Bluey.

'I think we should return to the subject of our leopard,' said Dr Drexler sternly.

Amazon was delighted to do so. 'Just one leopard?' she said. 'It seems rather a long way to go . . .'

'You don't quite understand,' Dr Drexler continued impatiently. 'There are only thirty or so Amur leopards left in the wild. Think of that. And there's a suggestion that the leopard is a female – she may have cubs. It is common for them to have two in a litter. If that's the case then ten per cent of the world's wild population of the Amur leopard has been trapped by that fire.'

'So we fly in there, get the cats out, take them somewhere safe?' said Bluey.

Dr Drexler took off his spectacles and cleaned them with his spotless white handkerchief. 'That, in, *ah*, essence, is the, er, long and the short of it.'

'Wait,' said Amazon. 'Are you saying you want *me* to go to Siberia to help save this leopard?'

'Our team,' continued Dr Drexler, still cleaning his glasses, 'is somewhat stretched at the moment. We've got a team out in Mozambique and another in Guatemala. Believe me, if there was an alternative, I'd take it. Do you think you're, *ah*, up to it?'

Before Dr Drexler could put his glasses back on, Amazon had leapt out of bed.

'I do believe that's a yes,' said Frazer.

Amazon froze. 'But my parents . . . I almost forgot . . . Is there any news?'

'Not yet, I'm afraid. But Mr Hunt – Hal Hunt, that is – has called in from Vancouver saying he has a number of leads. He actually suggested that it would be good to get you involved in the leopard rescue to help take your mind off . . . things.'

'So who's in the team?' asked Bluey.

'As I said, you three are all we can spare. Miss Coverdale, you'll be heading up the expedition. You've been out there before, so you know what to expect.'

'So you won't be coming?' asked Miranda.

'No, Mr Hunt has asked me to stay on here with a skeleton crew. You'll be met at Vladivostok by a Russian, Boris Lunakarski.'

'This is sooooooo coooooooooool!' said Frazer.

Amazon rolled her eyes, but still felt the excitement surging inside her.

'Right,' said Dr Drexler, 'let's get you kitted out – you leave tonight.'

That afternoon, Amazon asked Frazer if she could have a go on the X-Ark.

'I reckon it's the least you owe me,' she said, and Frazer had to agree.

Frazer showed Amazon how to load the darts, and then he lined up some tin cans on a fence about ten metres away.

'You have to allow for any wind that's blowing. And the dart begins to dip after a –'

Amazon didn't wait for him to finish. She pulled the trigger, and the middle can flew off the fence, struck by the dart.

Frazer stared at her open-mouthed.

'I-I-I –' was all he managed to say.

Amazon didn't tell him that she'd aimed for the left-hand can. The shot was a fluke. However, she had an advantage over Frazer: she'd actually bothered to read the thick manual that came with the gun. Therefore she knew that she now had to adjust the sights, using a little dial on the side.

The next two shots took out the other two cans.

Amazon handed the gun back to Frazer, thinking that she'd got her sweet revenge on her cousin.

13

Siberia Bound

Two days and six thousand miles later, Amazon and Frazer, along with Bluey and Miranda Coverdale, were climbing stiffly out of an ancient Antonov An-2 biplane into a field surrounded by the thickly forested mountains of the Sikhote-Alin range.

The journey had been long and gruelling. First came the overnight flight by Boeing 747 from New York to Seoul in South Korea. Amazon had sat next to Miranda, hoping that as the two girls on the expedition they could do some bonding. But Miranda never dropped her guard, and talked exclusively about the practicalities of the mission.

It was the first time she'd been in charge and, like everything else, she took her responsibility very seriously. Amazon fell asleep as Miranda was telling her all about the importance of genetic diversity in the leopard population.

From Seoul they took a tatty old Russian Tupolev airliner on to Vladivostok, the once great home port of the Russian navy, now shabby and down-at-heel.

The plane was full of noisy Russian families, passing around food and shouting for attention from the grumpy stewards.

For their meal, they were each given an orange and a cracked plastic glass of black tea. When she looked in the seat pocket for a copy of the safety instructions, Amazon found something hairy. At first she thought it was a dead mouse, but then decided that it was more likely to be a long-abandoned orange that had grown a coat of furry fungus.

The passengers held their collective breath as the Tupolev began its descent, and then clapped and cheered when the plane bumped down safely at Vladivostok.

They were met in the shiny new terminal building by a giant Russian with untidy black hair and a moustache that looked bushy enough in which to hide a whole family of Amur leopards.

He strode up to them saying, in a voice that boomed like the end of the earth, 'You call me Boris. Is not my real name, but you Americans like to call all Russians "Boris". Am I right? Yes I am.'

As Amazon and Frazer were to find out, Boris liked to answer his own questions.

'Where is man in charge?'

'Here. I mean, I am in charge,' said Miranda, stepping forward.

The Russian stared at Miranda, and then at the

others, before breaking into a broad smile, showing a random collection of gold and black teeth.

'Is American joke, yes? How is lady in charge? Job here not to make cake or go shopping for shoe, but to catch deadly animal which enjoy kill people.'

Whatever it was that Miranda said to the giant – speaking in fluent Russian and with a tone that was sharp enough to cut through sheet metal – Amazon would never find out. But it was enough to make Boris hold up his hands in mock surrender.

'OK, OK,' he said. 'So you is boss. Boris just here to help save leopard, tiger, whatever. But I think American lady more fierce than leopard and tiger.' Then he bent down and said to Amazon, 'You, little American girl, have you learned to be like tiger yet?'

'I'm not an American,' said Amazon rather snootily. 'I'm English.'

'Ah good. Then you be my very nice little English friend.' The Russian picked her up as easily as you'd pick up a pencil. 'I, Boris, protect you from all, for favourite food of leopard and tiger, is little girl. Also save from bear and wolf, who only eat little girl if nothing better, haha!'

Amazon squirmed out of his hairy-fingered grasp.

'I don't need protecting, thank you very much.'

'That we see,' said Boris. 'You all follow now.'

'I kinda like this guy,' said Frazer as they trailed behind the giant.

'He's certainly a character,' said Bluey.

'So was Ivan the Terrible,' said Amazon.

Frazer snorted, 'I say we call him Boris the Bad.'

'Let's cut that out, guys,' said Miranda. 'He may be a clown, but Dr Drexler briefed me that Boris Lunakarski is a key man down here. He's one of the main links between the conservationists and the regional government. Without him, nothing gets done. It's not a good situation, but that's the way it is.'

'ALSO, BORIS NOT DEAF AND SPEAK ENGLISH GOOD!' bellowed Boris without bothering to turn round.

14

A Hairy Flight

The An-2 and its pilot were waiting for them in a remote corner of the airfield. The plane looked like something from an old movie or a museum of aviation history.

'This thing has got *way* too many wings,' said Frazer, looking at the biplane distrustfully. 'I didn't know you even got planes like that any more. Who's going to fly it, the Red Baron?'

'Is greatest aircraft in history of world,' boomed Boris. 'First fly in 1947. Sixty years ago and more. What American aircraft fly that long, eh? I tell you, diddly squat zero zilch, eh? Ha ha. After that long time American plane fall out of sky, like duck shot by I, Boris.'

A rickety metal ladder led up into the cluttered interior. The seats had all been ripped out to make space for cargo so the passengers had to sit on crates and boxes.

'Most irregular,' sighed Miranda, cleaning the top of a dusty case with her handkerchief.

Amazon wedged herself on the floor between her rucksack and a metal cage. She thought the cage was empty, until something in it hissed angrily.

'Keep fingers out of cage,' said Boris. 'Unless you think nine fingers better than ten, ha ha.'

Amazon pulled her hand away from the wire, but not before her fingers had brushed something so soft it felt like warm air. The two creatures inside looked almost like otters.

'What are they?'

'Is sable,' said Boris. 'We take to release in mountains. Not many left because nice fur make best coat for Russian winter.'

Miranda pulled a sour face. 'The best coat for a sable, you mean.'

'Sure. Is just what Boris mean,' replied the Russian, rolling his black eyes. 'Now fasten seat belts, ha ha. See joke is NO SEAT BELTS!'

'Funny guy,' said Amazon, without smiling.

The Antonov trundled slowly along the runway, and laboured into the sky, only just climbing over the electricity lines at the end of the field. The old plane was seriously overloaded: as well as the team and their equipment, there were other mysterious boxes and packages belonging to Boris. The plane lurched and plunged at random, and the engines whined like hungry dogs. It was so noisy in the cabin that conversation was almost impossible, although it didn't stop Boris from bellowing out Russian songs between mouthfuls of the very large, very smelly garlic sausage he was munching on. He offered Amazon a bite.

'No thanks,' she said, trying not to retch.

Then Boris reached into his jacket and pulled out a bottle of vodka. 'Must go say hello to my friend, pilot. Flying airplane thirsty work, eh?'

He clambered heavily through the crowded fuselage, and disappeared through the door into the cockpit.

Amazon was fascinated by the pair of sables. Their coats were a lovely rich velvety brown, and she desperately wanted to push her face into the softness. She found a piece of sausage, dropped by Boris, and poked it through the wire at the front of the cage. One of the sables sniffed it suspiciously and then nibbled. It seemed to like it and came back for more.

'Sorry, little guy,' said Amazon. 'Nothing left.' But she did risk touching again that luxurious fur and, rather than biting her finger off, the sable rubbed itself against her.

'You definitely have a way with animals, don't you,' Frazer shouted.

Amazon smiled back, and shrugged.

Apart from making friends with the sable, the one reward of the dangerous flight was the view out of

the small window. It was so beautiful it almost took Amazon's mind off the lack of comfort, the stench of Boris's horrible sausage and the fear of imminent death. Thickly wooded hills rolled away as far as the eye could see. The hills were cut by rivers – some wide and brown and lazy, others raging with a white intensity through narrow gorges.

Miranda leant over and shouted into Amazon's ear. 'You're looking at one of the most diverse and fertile environments on the planet.'

'I always thought Siberia was just endless frozen

plains with nothing alive except, I don't know, reindeer or something.'

'Technically this region is known as the Russian Far East, rather than Siberia. The Siberia you're thinking of does exist, but further north and east. Don't get me wrong, the winters here are pretty grim – long nights, freezing winds, lots of snow. But the summers can be quite warm. This is one of the last great forest wildernesses.'

Boris re-emerged from the cockpit.

'Pilot OK now for landing,' he announced loudly. 'Without vodka he would never have courage, ha ha!'

On cue, the Antonov began to descend in a series of stomach-churning lurches. Amazon reached out and grabbed Miranda's hand. Miranda looked at her quizzically for a moment, and then gave the hand a quick squeeze.

'Don't worry,' she said. 'These guys may appear to be oafs, but they're professionals, and they've made this trip hundreds of times.'

It was late afternoon when the old plane finally bumped down on to a rough airfield on a narrow strip of flat ground between the hills.

15

Meeting the Team

Two battered Russian jeeps pulled up beside them as they were unloading their gear. A tall, thin guy with a straggly beard and dark shadows under his eyes climbed out of one of the jeeps and walked towards them with a gangly, awkward stride. He reminded Amazon, for some reason, of a sad ostrich.

The driver of the other jeep – a compact, bullet-headed man wearing sunglasses – got out, but leant against the bonnet, his face hard and blank.

'Good to see you again, Bob,' said Miranda, shaking the hand of the bearded man.

'You too, Miranda,' Bob replied, looking a little distracted. His face was long and haggard. He strained his thin neck to look round them towards the plane.

'Is Doctor Drexler still with the others in the aircraft?'

'Doctor Drexler isn't here,' said Miranda. 'He had

to stay back at the TRACKS base. And I'm afraid there are no "others".'

'You mean this is it?'

'It's all we could spare.'

'But these are just . . . kids!'

'Hey, I'm twenty-one years old!' said Bluey.

'OK, fine, but these two here . . .' He waved his hand towards Amazon and Frazer. 'I mean *literally* kids. Do you realize how serious the situation is? Or how dangerous? There are six kinds of deadly animal in these woods: the biggest tigers in the world, brown bears fiercer than any grizzly, black bears, wolves and, of course, the leopards. And there's something more dangerous than any tiger or leopard –'

Boris strode forward – he was no taller than Bob, but nevertheless seemed to dwarf him. 'I, Boris, protect these children from tiger with bare hands, ha ha!'

'In case you've forgotten, Boris,' said Bob, 'our job here is to protect leopards and tigers, not children.'

'Look, mister,' said Frazer, putting his hands on his hips and standing with his legs apart. 'I don't know who you are, but I'm the son of Hal Hunt, and I've been rescuing animals since I was seven years old. I've swum with sharks in the South China Sea, been dive-bombed by eagles on top of a volcano in Panama and had a bear chase me up a tree in Alaska. This girl here is my cousin, Amazon, and she's as smart as a whip and about as tough as a kid could be, and just about the best natural shot with a tranq gun I've ever seen. The reason we're both here is because *my* dad's looking for *her* dad, and so there was no one else to come. But if you think you can do without us then we'll get back on the plane and fly home again. And, anyway, just who the heck are *you*?'

The man stared hard at Frazer and Amazon and then laughed, for what looked like the first time in many months. Possibly years.

'Sorry,' he said, still smiling. 'It's been a difficult week. And I guess you guys *are* paying the bills round here. So, as long as you know what you're letting yourselves in for . . .'

'We quite understand,' said Miranda firmly.

'Dead right,' said Bluey. 'It's what we're all about.'

'Team,' Miranda continued, 'let me introduce you. This is Bob Doolins – he's probably the world's greatest living expert on the Amur leopard, and he isn't always this grumpy. He helped to stabilize the leopard population down in Southwest Primorye, and now he's spearheading the project to reintroduce it into this part of the Sikhote-Alin range. Nobody knows more about the leopard than this man. So how's it going, Bob?'

'To tell the truth, things are not so good here, Miranda,' said Doolins. 'We've got fire and poachers and who knows what else. But let's get your gear loaded up and I'll brief you properly when we get

60

back to the camp. We're temporarily staying with the family of a local hunter and trapper called Makha, who's acting as our guide. He lives with his wife, who I warn you is a rather fearsome old lady, and his grandson.'

'Hunter . . .?' said Amazon suspiciously. 'I thought the hunters were the enemy?'

'Take it easy,' said Doolins. 'It's complicated . . . Let's move it out.'

16

Setting Free the Sables

It took them three hours to drive to the house of the hunter, bumping over rutted tracks that were so narrow the branches of the trees slapped like bony fingers at the jeep windows. Frazer and Amazon were in the back of the jeep driven by the quiet Russian in sunglasses. Bluey was in the front passenger seat.

'I am Kirov,' the driver said when they set off, and that was all.

Amazon looked at Frazer and Frazer looked at Amazon, and they both fought the urge to giggle. But the laughter they swallowed down had more tension in it than happiness. There was something unsettling about the man: a vague feeling of danger, quite different from the bluster and bustle of Boris.

Bluey twisted round in the seat to talk to them.

'Don't get the wrong idea about Bob Doolins – I've heard a lot about him from the other Trackers, and the word is that he really is a great guy. The thing is he's been out here a long time more or less on his own, and I think the pressure gets to him. Lots of people want our leopards dead, and the responsibility all falls on his shoulders.'

'Fine,' said Amazon, 'but he could have given us a chance. I was always taught that it was good manners to hold off judging people until you've seen what they can do.'

Now it was the turn of Bluey and Frazer to look at each other, suppressing smiles.

'What are you two smirking at?' she said. 'OK, OK, so maybe I don't always practise what I preach. But I'm learning.'

Amazon was hoping that the drive would be as spectacular as the flight over the mountains, but the trees closed in on either side and so she saw nothing but the earth-dark trunks and the still-deeper darkness at the forest's heart. At one moment she thought she saw something striped in the undergrowth, but it was just a last ray of early-evening sunlight piercing the canopy.

After an hour the jeep in front of them stopped, and Boris got out, carrying the sable cage. Amazon leapt out to join him. She wanted to see the beautiful little creatures get their freedom.

Boris carried the cage a little way into the forest, and Amazon joined him. It was her first real experience of the wilderness. It was intensely quiet, but the silence had a sort of watchful quality, as if the world were just waiting for her to go before it resumed its bustling activity.

Boris looked at her and grunted, as if to say, 'Oh, you?' Then he set the cage down and opened the door, murmuring softly in Russian to the animals.

'What are you saying?' Amazon asked.

'I say "run away and make some more little fur coats for rich ladies".'

Amazon ignored him, and crouched down next to the cage. The sables nervously sniffed at the air, and then suddenly shot out. One disappeared straight into the tangled undergrowth, moving its short legs and sinuous body with a lithe grace that took Amazon's breath away. The other sable, however, stopped and turned. To her delight, it ran back to her, and let her indulge in one luxurious stroke along the whole length of its coat. It was like putting her hand in liquid silk. And then, with a chittering cry, the sable went to join its partner.

Boris looked at her strangely. 'Never seen that before,' he said, and then turned to go back to the jeeps.

17

Frazer Attacked!

It was almost dark by the time they reached their destination. The house was nothing more than a rough cabin in a clearing, with trees closing in on every side. There were a few outbuildings in various states of decay. It looked as though it was perhaps once a bigger settlement – a small village, even. But now it was lonely and desolate.

The track they had been driving along ended here.

'Looks like this is quite literally the end of the road,' said Frazer.

In reply, Kirov made a low grunt. He had, at least, taken off his sunglasses in the gathering gloom. His eyes were pale blue and gave nothing away about the soul within.

Frazer climbed out of the jeep, desperate to stretch his legs after the long drive. Just as his feet touched the soft earth, he heard a frantic pounding of paws and a panting of breath. He looked up, and saw a black shape come bounding out towards him from the dark of the woods.

It was a creature of shadow, something that drew the night around itself until the very darkness became flesh. Frazer thought he saw the eyes flash, thought he could see the glint of frothing saliva on the beast's savage lips. He saw, in an instant, that a tiger or bear was about to end his career as a Tracker just when it was getting to be fun.

Well, he was going to go down fighting. There was no time to get the X-Ark or even his pocket knife, but he clenched his fists, as if he were about to take part in a break-time brawl at school. Despite his courage, he could not fight his own body's urge to cringe back, and to close his eyes.

'Down, Boris, stupid beast.'

Frazer opened his eyes and saw Boris clutching at the spiked collar of an enormous black dog. Despite its size, the creature squirmed and writhed at the big Russian's feet, and Frazer couldn't tell if it was terror or simply that grovelling joy you sometimes see in dogs when they greet their masters after a long separation.

'This Boris dog, Boris,' bellowed the Russian. 'He is finest hunting dog in Russia, probably world.'

Frazer sprang forward, relieved he hadn't screamed. Had anyone even noticed his terror? He particularly hoped that Amazon hadn't . . .

'Yeah, I knew it was a dog,' he babbled. 'Anyone could see it was just a dog. Good boy,' he added,

reaching his hand out to the beast, then withdrawing it again when it was met with a snarl.

'Hang on,' said Amazon, coming round from her side of the jeep. 'Your dog's called Boris, Boris?'

Boris looked perplexed. 'What? No, dog not called Boris-Boris. Boris-Boris is stupid name for dog. Only idiot call dog Boris-Boris. Is this how you call dog in America?'

'No, I'm not from America! I meant to say . . . I just meant that it seems weird you've called your dog Boris, the same as you.'

'You forget, my name not really Boris. But I see how this can confuse tiny American mind, made soft with fast food and computer games.'

'So how are we going to tell you apart?' Amazon persisted. 'I mean, if someone says that Boris has to go walkies, how do we know if they mean the person or the dog?'

Boris looked very seriously at Amazon, which made it even harder for her not to laugh.

'Is good question. OK, when we say just "Boris" you all know it mean Boris, me, man of Russia. When we want Boris dog, then we say "Boris dog". Is clear?'

'Is clear,' said Frazer, who had got his cool back, and was pleased to have the chance to try out the comedy Boris voice he'd been practising. Amazon's giggle floated through the evening air.

18

The House of Makha

The cabin was made from logs of rough-hewn pine. Inside there was just a single large room, with an iron stove at one end. At the other end there was a raised platform, accessible by ladder.

At the stove was the hunched figure of an ancient woman. She was wearing a long smock made out of some kind of leather, which had an almost scaly sheen to it, and her weathered face was curiously oriental.

The old woman turned to stare at the new arrivals. She peered at them through small black eyes, which were deeply hidden in the folds and wrinkles of her leathery face. She made a strange gesture with her hand, almost as though she were performing some blessing or curse, and muttered to herself in a language that Amazon could tell was not Russian. It made the hairs stand up on the back of her neck. And then, with a grunt, the old lady returned to the huge iron pot she was stirring with a wooden spoon as big as an oar.

Amazon and Frazer looked at each other. 'I suddenly feel like we're in a fairy story,' Amazon whispered.

'Yeah,' agreed Frazer, 'one of those scary ones where the witch eats the kids. Just remember to poke a stick out of the bars of the cage so she still thinks you need fattening up.'

'Boy is right,' rumbled Boris, who'd overheard their words. 'Old crone is witch for sure – Russian name for this is *Baba-Yaga*. People who live here is barbarian savage. We call them fish-skin tartars, because they wear skin of fish for cloth. These people say prayer to tree, to sky, to rock, to fire – any old rubbish or figment of imagination. Even to tiger, eh, ha! They should clear off and leave woods to civilized man like Boris.'

'I don't like that kind of talk, Lunakarski,' said Bob Doolins, who had just come in. 'The Udege have lived in these forests for centuries before the Russians and Chinese came, so they have a far greater right to be here than you.'

Boris shrugged and walked away, waving his hand dismissively. 'Don't need no talk from Yankee about Russian forest.'

Doolins turned to Amazon and Frazer. 'He's only sounding off like that because the old woman's husband and grandson aren't here yet. They've been out scouting the area, checking for illegal trappers.'

'Who are these people?' Frazer asked. 'What did you call them . . . *Oo-duh-gay*?'

'That's right. The family who live here are part of a group called the Udege. They are related to a number of other native tribes – the Nanai, and the Ulch.'

'They look kind of Chinese . . .'

'They do originally come from Manchuria in northern China, but that was hundreds of years ago. There are less than two thousand of them left, and only a handful still speak the Udege language and keep the old ways alive.'

'But they're hunters,' said Amazon. 'How can that be good? Don't they kill the tigers and leopards?'

'No. That oaf Lunakarski was right about one thing: the Udege have great respect for the tiger, in particular, and they would only ever harm one to save their own lives. It's true, though, that they are some of the finest hunters and trackers in the world, and that the animals they hunt – deer and wild pigs, mainly – are also the prey of the tigers and leopards. But they never take more than they need to survive, and they respect the spirit of the place and the animals they kill. The real threat up here isn't the Udege or any of the other native groups – it's the hunters who kill to order for Chinese medicine, and the loggers who destroy the forest.'

He was interrupted by Bluey, who burst in carrying bags and packs from the jeep. He glanced around the cabin.

'It's a bit rough and ready, guys,' he said. 'But I guess we'll look on this as the lap of luxury when we've been out in the forest for a few days.'

19

The Rescue Plan

With the arrival of Bluey, Bob Doolins cleared his throat loudly and said, 'Can I have your attention, please. We really don't have any time to waste.'

He was standing in front of a large map pinned to the wall of the cabin. Amazon, Frazer, Miranda, Bluey, Kirov and Boris all gathered round.

'This is the situation,' continued Doolins. 'On the western side of the Sikhote-Alin mountain range most of the rivers either drain into the basin of Lake Khanka, down here, or they flow further north to meet the Amur River.'

He used a wooden stick to point first to a big blue splodge that marked the enormous Lake Khanka, and then to a long blue line of the Amur, snaking over thousands of miles across Russia to the Sea of Japan.

'One of the major tributaries of the Amur is the Ussuri, which rises here in the mountains. The

Ussuri is itself a pretty serious waterway, and has its own tributaries. He pointed again at the map. 'At this point, the Ussuri is joined by the River Khor. You can see how the two rivers gradually approach each other, forming this funnel-shaped area of land. It's almost like a long, thin island . . .'

'But not really an island,' said Frazer. 'There's no water at the top end. So stuff – animals, I mean, can just walk out of there.'

He got up and pointed to the open forest indicated on the map.

'You got it, son,' said Doolins. 'Normally animals – and people – can get in and out through that gap. But the gap has been closed, trapping everything between the two rivers.'

'The fire,' said Amazon.

'That's right, young lady, the fire.' Doolins looked to Kirov. 'Viktor, perhaps you could explain this part.'

The silent Kirov stood up and took the wooden pointer from Doolins. He spoke quietly, but in perfectly good English, which surprised Amazon and Frazer.

'A forest fire has been started, and it now stretches from here to here, trapping everything between the rivers, like a cork in a bottle. The fire is moving down the mountain, pushing all animals in front of it. But soon it will reach the end where the rivers meet.'

Suddenly Amazon saw the urgency of the situation. 'The animals will be able to swim across the river, won't they . . .?'

Boris guffawed. 'Ha, little English girl think of little English river, babbling brook, tinkling stream, ha ha. Ussuri and Khor is proper Russian rivers: it is torrent, it crash, it foam white. Swim in Ussuri and you end up dead as dormouse, as you English say, yes?'

'Actually,' said Doolins, taking over again, 'some animals may be able to escape across the river. Tigers are good swimmers, some of the larger species of deer may be able to make it . . .'

'And leopards?' asked Frazer.

'Leopards? No, not so good. And, as you may have heard, we have reason to believe that the leopard we are seeking has two small cubs, so the river is not an option. That's why you're here – to help us to track, tranq and save the leopards. As the leader of the TRACKS team, do you have anything to add, Ms Coverdale?'

'Just a question. Kirov said that a fire had been started. Did he mean *deliberately*?'

Doolins paused for a moment to consider before answering. 'Fires are common further south, where the forest is drier in the summer. But not here. Which is why we think it was started deliberately.'

'Who by?' asked Miranda.

Kirov answered. 'Probably hunters. They use the fires to force the animals into a smaller and smaller area. They sell bones and skin to China and Korea for medicine. And they kill bears for their gall bladder, also used in medicine.'

'And leopards?'

'Yes, kill leopard for the bones, and for the skin. A man could earn from one leopard what he would earn in a year of working on a farm.'

'And you know for certain that the hunters are in the pocket of land now?' asked Miranda.

Kirov shrugged. 'Makha and his grandson are looking now. If they are there, Makha will find them.'

'Thank you, Viktor,' said Doolins. 'And there is another factor. All of this land is protected because of the leopard reintroduction programme. If we lose the leopards, then the local government may well sell off the land to other interests. Is that correct, Boris?'

Boris did one of his shrugs – like everything else about him, Boris's shrugs were huge. 'Of course. Government is corrupt. It sell anything it can to make the men at the top rich. It is the way out here.'

'So, as you see,' Doolins continued, 'there is no time to lose. We start in the morning. I'll be coordinating the fire-fighting effort. The fire-fighters on the site aren't professionals – they're just Russian troops the Interior Ministry has allocated to us, and they're a pretty undisciplined lot. The rest of you will split into three teams to go after the leopards.

It's your call, Miranda, but I suggest that the two youngsters go with the Udege – they know these forests better than anyone, and they will keep them safe. I take it you have tranquillizer guns?'

'Sure do!' said Frazer, tapping the aluminium case. 'I've got my X-Ark right here.'

Bluey chuckled. 'If I was Amazon's rear end, I'd be afraid, very afraid.'

'Ha ha,' said Frazer. 'I've already explained that it was all part of my brilliant plan. And the chance of me needing to shoot Amazon in the butt again is pretty slim.'

Doolins ignored the jokes. 'The mother,' he said, 'has a radio collar, so you may be able to track her using radio receivers. You've brought extra sets, right?'

'Sure have,' said Bluey. 'Three.'

'Right, then,' said Doolins, 'if there are no more questions, let's turn in.'

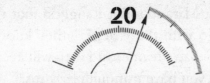

20

'I'll Take My Chances
with the Tigers'

'Turn in where?' asked Frazer, looking around the hut for a place to sleep.

'Up on the platform,' said Doolins. 'I'm afraid there's not much privacy.'

'Erm . . . that reminds me,' said Amazon, a little sheepishly. 'Where's the loo?'

'What is "loo"?' said Boris, butting in where he really wasn't wanted.

'The . . . the, ah, little girls' room . . .'

Boris shrugged, mystified.

'She means the, ah . . .' Bluey tried, but got stuck.

Kirov said something in Russian, and Boris burst into his titanic laughter.

'Ah, Boris understand.'

He disappeared outside for a moment, and came back carrying something.

'Here is spade, out there is woods.'

'You are kidding!' Amazon gasped.

'What, Russian woods not good enough for English girl?'

'What about the bears and the tigers . . .'

'English girl safe – they not look. Russian animals very polite, ha ha. No, only joke. If bear come, girl shout for help. If tiger come, don't bother shout, already too late.'

'Do you want me to come and, erm . . . keep guard?' said Frazer.

'No way!' snapped Amazon. 'I'll take my chances with the tigers.'

'OK, Lunakarski, enough of that,' said Doolins, although the corners of even his mouth were twitching. 'Amazon, there's a small shed with a chemical toilet out in the yard. I'll show you the way.'

Amazon blushed. She hated being tricked.

'No thanks, I'll find it myself. Can't be that hard.'

'OK, but take this,' said Doolins, and threw her a torch.

'And watch out for tiger, ha ha,' boomed Boris.

21

Terror in the Night

Amazon stepped out into what was now full night. It was good to escape the smoke and noise of the cabin. It was pitch black. If there was a moon, it was well hidden behind a thick layer of cloud. The stars were nowhere to be seen. Amazon had never known such darkness. Once the door to the cabin had swung shut behind her, she literally couldn't see her hand in front of her face.

She flicked on the torch and shone it on the solid wall of trees that circled the little collection of huts and shacks. The strong beam lit up the tree trunks surrounding the clearing, but could not penetrate into the impossible blackness beyond. She shivered, and hurried to the nearest of the huts, hoping that it would be the one with the loo. She scraped open the door, and something ran squeaking over her foot. Amazon had never been the sort of girl who was scared of mice and rats, but in her surprise she let out a scream.

The door to the cabin opened.

'Zonnie? Are you all right?' cried Frazer, silhouetted in the doorway.

He must have been right there, Amazon realized, waiting and listening to make sure she was safe.

'Of course I am,' she snapped.

'OK. Well, just shout if you want, er, company.'

Amazon pulled herself together. 'Yes, of course. I just love company in the bathroom.'

And then she felt that she'd been a bit mean. Frazer was only trying to help, after all. So she added: 'I'm fine. Just had a little rodent issue.'

'That's the woods for you,' said Frazer with a shrug. He turned to go back inside. 'Just yell if you, y'know, *need* anything.'

It turned out that Amazon wasn't even in the right shack. It was just a woodshed, piled with logs. She shone the torch around the yard and headed for another of the outbuildings. She opened the door warily, and felt around for the light switch, and then instantly felt stupid. There was, of course, no electric light.

The torch showed that it was a truly horrid place, thick with cobwebs, with a dankness in the air and a smell that Amazon hoped she'd never have to encounter again. But at least this time it was the *right* horrid place: there was the disgusting chemical toilet – just a plastic bucket with a flimsy seat.

And there, also, on the floor, was a huge shape, bristling and fierce.

This time Amazon swallowed her scream.

'I'm not afraid of you, Boris dog, dog of Boris,' she said. 'You're a big stupid coward.'

Boris the Dog looked at Amazon. She was right. He wasn't a very bright dog. Or a very brave one. He rather liked the look on the faces of humans when he ran up barking at them. Should he bark at this small one? It might be fun. But he also quite liked it when they scratched him behind the ear. He didn't get that often from his master, the giant hairy human. So up he got and pushed his face into Amazon's hand.

The thing is that Amazon loved all animals, even the big, stupid, smelly ones (Boris the Dog was responsible for at least part of the loo's nasty aroma). So she said: 'OK, softy,' and gave him the scratch he was after.

Boris the Dog made a wet sound and Amazon felt warm drool on her hand. 'Yuk,' she said. 'Thanks very much. Now get out and give a girl some privacy.'

She opened the loo door, shunted the dog outside, then shone the torch around again. She shuddered as beetles scurried away from the beam, and moths fluttered to it. Cobwebs as big as bed sheets draped themselves between the low roof and the flimsy walls. There was no window, but the loose planks that made up the walls had wide gaps. She peered through, and then sent a narrow finger of torchlight into the dark.

Nothing out there.

Then, as she turned away she thought that she caught some movement, just where the trees met the clearing. She spun back again, and forced herself to look.

Was it that idiotic dog? No, because Boris the Dog suddenly appeared, standing in the yard a metre in front of her. He was staring in the same direction as Amazon. Whatever it was that she had seen, the dog had seen it too. And now the big dog was whining and backing away.

That was not good.

Amazon peered into the darkness, concentrating so hard that her eyes ached. But no matter how hard she stared she could not make anything out. Then she saw that the dog's head was turning.

His finer senses detected what she could not see.

Whatever it was that lurked in the treeline was circling slowly. The dog was clearly terrified.

Amazon opened the door a sliver. 'Boris, get in here,' she hissed, 'and the dog leapt at the chance to squeeze in. It pressed itself up against her, shivering with terror.

'Oh, now I remember,' said Amazon to herself. 'Tigers and leopards both love to eat dogs.'

And then she dismissed the idea. A tiger or leopard wouldn't come so close to the house, would it? It was more likely to be a deer, or some other forest creature that had spooked the dog. She already knew what a coward he was. Perhaps it was even her own beautiful sables, come to say hello.

Except that the forest again had that silent watchfulness that she'd noticed before. And now there was an extra layer. Something thick and tangible and frightening.

Luckily, help was close at hand. She hated to come across as too girlie, but she wasn't a fool.

She opened the door a crack and yelled out.

'Guys, help! Frazer, Mr Doolins . . . There's something out here!'

But it was no use. From the cabin there came the raucous sound of Boris singing at the top of his voice.

She estimated the distance to the cabin. It was probably no more than fifteen metres. She peered again through the crack in the shed, and shone the light into the darkness.

And there, reflected back at her, were two unmistakable points of light.

Eyes.

Back home in England, Amazon had often seen the eerie light reflected in the eyes of a fox or a cat at night, and even then, when she knew that there was no danger, it had always given her a tiny shiver of fear.

But this was different. This was no fox. And the danger was real.

The eyes were wide set and, even though the wall of the shed came between them, Amazon knew that they were fixed on her. She felt the power and intelligence behind them. For the first time in her life she had come up against a creature that saw her as dinner.

And then the eyes blinked out.

Boris the Dog crushed even closer to Amazon, hiding his muzzle in the folds of her jumper.

'Stupid yellow-bellied dog,' she said, but how she also longed for someone bigger and braver than her, in whose jumper she could hide her own face.

She heard – or thought she heard – a twig snap. The tiger – if that's what it was – was now directly behind the toilet shed. The trees were perhaps three metres away – an easy leap for the greatest of the big cats. Was the flimsy hut strong enough to keep out a killer?

But Amazon was not the kind of girl to stand cowering and awaiting her fate.

'I don't know about you, Boris the Dog, but I have no intention of dying in a smelly outdoor lavatory. We're going to run for it. Understand?'

Just talking to the dog calmed Amazon a little.

Boris the Dog looked at her with his big foolish eyes.

'You wouldn't understand which end of a bone to chew, would you?' she said with a sigh. 'Well, never mind, just follow me.'

Amazon tensed herself, kicked open the door and sprinted. She was fast. She had easily won the hundred metres for her year at her school sports day. In a couple of seconds she was halfway to safety. Boris the Dog was slower from the starting blocks, but eventually the message got through to his small brain, and he galloped after her.

And, having got halfway, Amazon suddenly felt a little foolish. After all, it is so easy to imagine shapes in the dark. To imagine, even, the silver light of two feline eyes.

And then she felt it.

She couldn't even have said if by 'felt' she meant saw it, or heard it or even smelled it. But she knew it was there, and she knew that it was coming.

She lengthened her stride, willing her legs to go faster. And then a stray root caught her foot, and she fell sprawling on her face.

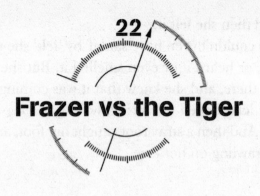

22

Frazer vs the Tiger

Frazer had watched Amazon leave the cabin with a vague feeling of unease. He didn't think that Bob and Miranda should have let her just go off on her own like that, even with a torch. Doolins had already gone on about the number of deadly animal species in the forest – how many was it? Six? Ten? No, not ten. But enough.

It added to his general feeling that something about this mission wasn't right. He was used to having more of the Trackers around. Bluey was great, of course, but he wasn't *that* experienced. Miranda Coverdale was incredibly efficient, even if she did have a look on her face like she'd just smelled something nasty – something nasty that she blamed on him.

But this was her first time as team leader.

And Bob Doolins looked like he was at the end of his tether – Frazer had never seen anyone look so tired.

The three of them were studying the map on the wall now.

And then there were the Russians. Boris was sort of amusing in his idiotic way, but Frazer knew that sometimes clever people could pretend to be idiots, if it suited their purpose.

Was Boris one of those fake idiots?

Or was he the real thing?

Either way, it was a touch worrying.

And, if Boris was a puzzle, the other Russian, Kirov, was even more mysterious. He was perfectly polite, but Frazer thought there was something he was keeping back. And Frazer had also noticed that he moved with a certain grace. The kind of grace you get with trained athletes.

Or soldiers.

The old witch he really didn't want to think about. He tried smiling at her. She smiled back. At least it might have been a smile, but it was hard to tell as she had not a tooth in her head, so it was like being smiled at by a frog.

A hungry-looking frog . . .

She licked her lips and pointed to the pot of black stew. What was she saying? That the stew was tasty? Or that he was going to end up in it, and she would very much enjoy eating him?

And now Boris had begun to sing. He was probably annoyed that no one was paying him any attention.

'*Kalinka, Kalinka . . .*' he sang, sounding like a village idiot blowing on a set of broken bagpipes.

And then Frazer thought he heard something else

– something from outside the cabin. A shout? Or just the cry of a bird?

'Guys,' he said to the group huddled over the map, 'did you hear –'

'Quiet, please, Frazer,' said Miranda without looking round. 'Can't you see we're planning the route for tomorrow? The last thing we need is to get lost.'

'But –'

'Tell me in five minutes.'

Frazer decided to go see – at least it would get him out of the crazy hut. At the last moment he grabbed the case holding the X-Ark, flicked it open, took out his pride and joy and slotted in one of the darts.

He opened the door and stepped out into the darkness and something black dashed past him, almost knocking him off his feet.

'What the –'

The dog.

Boris the dumb mutt.

It had bolted straight into the cabin, thumping through the half-open door.

And then, as he peered into the dark, he saw what was happening in the yard. Amazon was slowly picking herself up off the ground. She was staring fixedly behind her. Frazer followed the line of her gaze. And there he saw, shimmering in the gloom, like something from a dream, a tiger.

It couldn't be.

But it was.

It looked strangely confused, as if it didn't know what to do. Frazer had been in tricky situations before, though nothing quite like this. But he had to do something.

And that something involved the X-Ark.

Carefully he raised the tranq gun to his shoulder. It was a weird repeat of the whole giant-forest-hog incident. The thought came to him that if he hit Amazon again, this time nothing would save her – the tiger wasn't protecting its young, but stalking its prey.

And last time he'd aimed at the beast and hit the butt.

Should he aim at Amazon's butt, this time then? Was that his only hope of hitting the tiger?

Was it all because he hadn't set the sights properly? Maybe he shouldn't bother with the hi-tech sights at all, but go on instinct, like Luke Skywalker in *Star Wars*.

Yeah, that was it. He needed to go all Jedi. He needed the Force. He had to listen for the inner voice that would show him the way. He closed his eyes, and . . .

'No!'

He opened his eyes, and saw next to him a teenage boy. The boy was older than Frazer and Amazon, but he was a head shorter than either. He had the same oriental features as the old woman, but he was wearing jeans and a sweatshirt. Frazer guessed that this must be the grandson he'd heard about.

'My grandfather will fix this, I assure you,' he said. His English was oddly formal. The accent was strange, with hints of American mingling with the Russian, and other more exotic elements.

And then almost magically, it seemed to Frazer, a figure appeared out of thin air, materializing between Amazon and the tiger.

The Old Hunter

'Amba! Amba!'

Those were the only words that Amazon heard clearly. More words followed, some sounding harsh and scolding, some soft and almost pleading.

Amazon looked up from where she lay, cowering. What she saw was most strange. A short figure was standing in between her and the trees, facing the forest. His arms were open wide, and he held a heavy forked stick in one hand.

He was talking to something, although his stocky frame blocked Amazon's view, so she couldn't see what.

But she heard it. A low rumbling growl that flared up into a harsher roar.

And still the little man spoke to the tiger – for tiger surely it was. And as he spoke he moved slowly forward. And for the first time Amazon saw the creature.

It was magnificent. And terrifying. And truly, as

the moon momentarily appeared from behind the thick cloud, it did burn bright in that forest of the night.

Amazon could sense the huge power in its limbs, the strength of its jaws, the cunning hunter's intelligence that glittered in its eyes.

And yet, for all its concentrated power, it moved steadily backwards away from the little man. And Amazon sensed that the animal retreated not fearfully, but almost sulkily, as if it had been caught out doing something it knew was wrong.

And then Amazon realized what was so familiar in the man's tone of voice – he was telling it off! He was actually scolding the tiger, the way you would a naughty child. But also encouraging it to try harder to be good.

And it was wonderful, and almost funny. But then, just before the tiger reached the scrubby edge of the clearing, confusion descended.

Light and noise filled the space as the cabin door was thrown open, and then there came a bang that sounded to Amazon like a bomb going off in her own head. There was a snarling roar from the tiger – a roar this time not of threat, but of pain, and suddenly it was no longer there. It had passed through the wall of trees like a flame.

The little man turned, and Amazon saw the murderous black look on his face. She felt it, almost like a physical force, as if someone had slapped her.

And then she was surrounded by noise and bustle and concerned voices.

'Zonnie, you OK?' asked Frazer, helping her to her feet. 'I had you covered with the X-Ark, but then this guy appeared . . .' He gestured at the teenage stranger.

'What's happened? What's been going on?' said Miranda.

'Is easy,' said Boris, towering over them all. He was carrying a rifle. 'Tiger come for girl. Boris, he save life. Is no need to thank. Is Boris job.'

'You had no right to fire at the tiger,' said Bob Doolins with quiet rage.

Boris spat on the ground. 'Eh? What more important – life of tiger or life of English girl? Not even crazy man like you can think this, that animal is worth more than person. Anyway, if Boris fire at tiger then tiger would be dead. Boris just frighten.'

'Hey, my life wasn't in danger, and as I've already told you, I'm not –'

Amazon never finished her sentence. The rage of the little man – who truly had saved Amazon's life (or so she thought) – was not at all quiet. He stormed up to the giant Russian and shoved him squarely in the chest. The man was old – as old as the old lady in the cabin – and Boris was huge and powerful, but still the push left the Russian on his back, staring at the black sky.

Harsh words came with the shove. Again the only one that Amazon could make out clearly was 'Amba'.

Boris's face now was twisted with fury and humiliation. The rifle was still in his hand. He brought it to bear on the old man who stood over him. The man laughed, mockingly, and spoke again.

Boris's finger was on the trigger.

Amazon was horrified.

Everything had happened so quickly – one moment she was running for her life from the unseen hunter, and the next her saviour was about to be shot.

She shouted out, 'No!'

The teenage boy made as if to move towards Boris to protect his grandfather. Kirov half crouched, ready to spring into action, but whether that was to attack or defend Boris, Amazon didn't know.

But it was Frazer who stopped it.

'Put the gun down,' he said, walking forward and pointing the X-Ark at Boris.

The Russian looked at the tranq gun and grunted: 'Hrmmph. Is toy gun. Boris not impressed.'

In fact, Boris was right not to be impressed. Frazer was bluffing. The safety catch was firmly on and, even if it hadn't been, the boy was too well trained by his father to fire deliberately at a person. But once the bluff had begun Frazer had to go with it. Using every fragment of his acting talent, he said: 'You want me to shoot a dart into your eye, Boris? Because my guess is that it would smart a little. And the chances are it would burst your eyeball and splash the jelly all over your face. But hey,' he added, switching to his Boris voice, 'who needs two eyes anyway?'

'This a mistake you make, boy,' Boris growled, and just as Frazer had found a new coolness, so Boris had lost his bluster and rough humour, exposing something cold and hard beneath.

It was unclear how it would all turn out. The old man, still furious, glared at Boris. Boris, his moustache bristling, faced Frazer. And Frazer had the X-Ark trained on the Russian's eyeball.

And then near-tragedy turned into full-blown comedy. The old woman had followed the others from the cabin. She began to harangue the old man with words of extraordinary violence.

And nor did she stop at words. The big wooden spoon that she had been using to stir the frightful brown stew was now employed to wallop her husband over the head and shoulders. He tried to fend off her blows with his arms, but it was like trying to ward off a swarm of angry bees. He ran into the cabin, the old woman in hot, if rather arthritic, pursuit.

It was impossible not to laugh. And everyone did, except for Boris. His finger was still on the trigger of his rifle.

It was Kirov who went over to him and calmly took the weapon from his hands, saying a few quiet words in Russian, to which Boris, for once, had no answer.

'I think we go and eat,' Kirov said aloud to everyone. 'Plus, it is not so good to stay out here. Tiger is angry.'

'Good idea,' said Doolins, and they all retreated to the cabin.

25

A Dinner of Dog

Back inside the cabin, they sat down to a very awkward meal. The old woman served up the brown stew in heavy bowls, accompanied by black bread.

Boris sat hunched in a corner, chewing on his garlic sausage.

'Boris not eat dog,' he said.

'Dog?' said Amazon, staring in dismay at her bowl.

'Relax,' said Doolins. 'It's not dog, it's racoon dog –'

'Racoon!' spluttered Frazer.

'*Racoon dog*. It's not a racoon or a dog, but a separate species. They're quite common here, and the local people have always hunted them for their meat and skins. You should try it.'

'I'm vegetarian,' said Amazon and Frazer at the same time, although Amazon knew that Frazer was lying.

The teenage grandson of the old trapper looked on all this with an amused smile.

'My name is Dersu,' he said, bowing slightly to Amazon. 'I am very pleased to meet you. My apologies for the earlier disturbance.'

Just like Frazer, Amazon was struck by the strange formality of the boy's way of speaking, and his distinct graveness.

'Hi, Dersu,' she replied, shaking his hand. 'I'm Amazon and this chump here is Frazer –'

'Hey, chump yourself!'

Amazon ignored Frazer's interruption. 'And please don't apologize – I'm pretty sure that your grandfather saved my life back there. What was he doing? I mean he seemed to be talking to the tiger . . .'

'Yes, my grandfather is a famous shaman and has some strange beliefs about the tiger that I do not completely share. And sometimes he believes two different things at the same time. So he believes that the tiger – Amba, in our language – is a Great Spirit, a god, if you like. But he also believes that the tiger is the guard dog of the evil spirit that lives in the rocks overlooking the river.'

'*OK*,' said Frazer. 'So which tiger was that – the Great Spirit or the evil guard dog?'

'In some ways now it does not matter. When that stupid Russian fired at the tiger, he made it our enemy. Now my grandfather thinks it will not rest until it has killed us all or driven us out of its territory. He is very distressed.'

'How come you speak such good English?' asked Frazer in his usual direct way.

Dersu was quiet for a moment. 'My father earned enough money to send me to the American school in Moscow.'

'Oh,' said Amazon. 'I was going to ask you where your mum and dad are . . .'

'My mother died after I went away to the school.'

'Oh, I'm so sorry.'

'And your father?' asked Frazer.

Dersu looked down. 'I do not wish to say. It brings me shame.'

Frazer made as if to ask him more about this, but Amazon put a hand on his arm, and shook her head. The message was clear: *don't go there.*

Luckily, at that moment they were distracted by the old woman. She was holding something in her gnarled hands. It seemed to be a wooden doll of some kind. The face was long, and the eyes were made of small blue beads. It had no arms and the legs were bent.

As Amazon and Frazer watched, fascinated, the old woman tied string round the idol's neck, and then suspended it in front of the stove. She then threw some thick, waxy green leaves on the flames. The leaves shrivelled and burned, and their smoke filled the room with a heavy scent, not unpleasant – almost like rosemary, but somehow drowsy.

'What on earth is your grandmother doing?' asked Frazer.

'It's to protect the home,' said Dersu. 'So Amba does not come in.'

Amazon and Frazer exchanged looks. Frazer mouthed a word at her.

'*VOODOO*.'

'The wooden man is Kasalyanku,' Dersu continued. 'The leaves are a plant called ledum. They give Kasalyanku strength. He will protect us from Amba. This is the belief of my grandmother and grandfather.'

The old woman began to sing in a low voice, and suddenly the whole room was watching her in utter silence. As she sang, Makha accompanied her on a small drum. Her song faded out, as it had faded in, and even though she didn't believe in the power of such magic, the hairs on the back of Amazon's neck still stood up.

That night was not a comfortable one. After the meal Amazon and Frazer lay down on the hard floor in their sleeping bags. The adults talked for a while, and Amazon heard the chink of Boris's vodka bottle. But eventually quiet fell on the hut.

It was short-lived – Boris, predictably, started to snore.

'You awake?' whispered Frazer to Amazon.

'No,' said Amazon. 'I'm fast asleep.'

'Sounds like a truck crashing into a train and then they both roll off the side of the mountain.'

'Nah – sounds more like a tiger and a bear having a fight to the death.'

'And now the leopard's joined in. This is getting ugly.'

They giggled quietly. Then Frazer asked in a more serious voice, 'So how are you doing, Zonnie? I mean, I'm kind of used to all this, as I've been on missions before, but I guess it's all pretty strange for you.'

'Well,' replied Amazon, 'it's certainly a long way from England . . . but the truth is I'm loving it. I just wish I knew what was going on with my mum and dad.'

'They'll be fine. I know it. My dad'll save them. Oh, er, not that they need saving or anything. I just, er . . .'

'Fraze?'

'Yeah?'

'Be quiet and go to sleep.'

And eventually they both drifted off, unaware of the killer pacing impatiently outside.

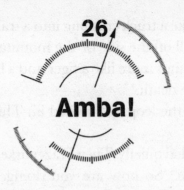

26

Amba!

The wound was more to Amba's pride than to his body, but the pain was, nevertheless, intense. The bullet from Boris's rifle had passed between his ears, singeing the short fur on his forehead, and then it clipped off the very tip of his tail. It drew just a drop or two of blood, but tigers very much dislike having the tips of their tails tweaked. Amba retreated into the forest, lay under a rotten log, licked his wound and brooded.

There was a memory, a good memory, and Amba sucked on it like a bone. Many years before he had turned the tables on a hunter who had been tracking him for days through the snowy forest. The presence of the human scared off the deer and other prey, and so, at last, Amba decided that this game must end.

The tiger lured the hunter along a track, then leapt from the path, doubled back through the trees and waited. The hunter, his eyes on the spoor in the snow, ignored the yapping of his dog, and knew nothing until Amba pounced. The yappy little dog made a fine dessert. All that was ever found of either was the hunter's gun and a single boot.

But Amba was not truly a man-eater. Man-eating tigers are almost always old and weak individuals with broken teeth and worn claws, who cannot hunt their usual prey. Amba did not savour the flesh of the strange animal that walked on two legs. And he was still strong enough to take on anything alive in the forest: the bristling boars, the black bears, even the mighty brown Ussuri bears – he'd eaten them all in his time, as well as his preferred sika deer. Oh yes, and plenty more dogs. Dogs were good to eat, and easy to catch.

It was the dog that he was really after at the place of the wooden caves. The small human was just an annoyance. But then the Old One had come. And Amba feared the Old One. He feared him because the Old One *knew*, and to be known is the great dread of the tiger.

And then the other human – the big one – had hurt him. And Amba did not forget being hurt.

So, after he had licked and brooded, he prowled back to the wooden cave, thinking that if any human came through the mouth of the cave then he would assuredly eat it.

And three times he paced round the clearing. But there was a smell he did not like, and a feeling that this was not, after all, a good place for a tiger. It made

Amba's tail hurt to be here, and so he padded away, cursing tiger curses.

But he still wanted vengeance. He wanted to inflict pain and death on an enemy. For a long time here in the north the only real foe for a tiger was the bear. But now there was a new rival. Smaller, but cunning. And Amba would brook no rival. He knew where the leopard was.

And her cubs.

Yes, he would kill the mother and then he would kill the cubs. Perhaps that would make the pain go away.

Awkward to get to, of course. He had already left the place of the fire once. He'd have to swim to get back. But it would be worth it.

Something deep in his soul told him that leopard was good to eat.

27
Gearing Up

Amazon woke the next morning with a stiff neck and a sore back. For the first time she missed – but only a little! – her hard bed and cold room back at Millbank Abbey.

The rest of the hut was already bustling with preparations for the hike. It was also the first time she got dressed into her expedition clothing: khaki lightweight trousers and a matching shirt, a breathable camouflage jacket and US Army issue jungle boots.

'I feel like I'm in some kind of a movie,' she said, checking her reflection in the window – there were no mirrors in the hut. 'I just don't know quite what kind . . .'

'You look cool,' said Frazer.

'You really should think of some word other than "cool" when you like something, you know,' said Amazon.

But she was secretly quite pleased.

They breakfasted on fried eggs, cooked by the

old woman, and hunks of black Russian bread.

After breakfast Amazon sat on the cabin porch and checked out her equipment. She had been issued with the standard TRACKS expedition backpack. It contained spare lightweight waterproof clothing, a fleece, a medical kit, a wash bag with soap, insect repellent, a water bottle, a tube of water-sterilizing tablets, a multi-tool, a tiny but powerful torch and emergency rations.

Amazon took everything out of the neat pack and then found she couldn't get it back in again. She heard an annoying chuckle and saw that Frazer was watching her. He sat next to her and helped her repack, showing her the best way to store everything.

'It's best if you keep it all in separate dry bags,' he said. 'Not just to keep it dry, but so you know where everything is. Nothing worse than having to empty the whole thing when all you need is an aspirin. And most people think you should put the heavy stuff at the bottom of the pack, but it's actually easier to trek if you keep the heavier things above your centre of gravity.'

'Who made you an expert?' asked Amazon, who didn't much like the way Frazer was suddenly acting like the boss of her.

'Five expeditions,' said Frazer. 'You learn the hard way.'

Amazon pulled a face and flicked Frazer's smug ear.

Miranda Coverdale came over and gave a small box to Amazon. 'This might come in handy. Make sure you learn how to use it.'

Amazon opened the box. Inside was a chunky green watch. It wasn't Amazon's style at all. She was about to say just that, but Frazer got in first.

'Cool . . . er, I mean, that's great,' he gushed. 'A GPS watch.' He looked up at Miranda. 'Where's mine?'

'Sorry, Frazer. Not after what happened with the satellite phone in Borneo.'

'Hey, that so wasn't my fault! What was I supposed to do – let the croc eat *me* instead of the phone?'

'That would have been considerably cheaper,' said Miranda, the merest hint of a smile pulling at the corners of her mouth. 'You're forming a team with Amazon, so you won't need two. And it's obvious that Amazon is much more reliable.'

'Not fair!' grumbled Frazer, and kicked over the rucksack he'd helped pack so neatly.

'Just remind me,' said Amazon. 'What exactly is a GPS watch?'

'See,' whined Frazer, 'she doesn't even know what it *is*!'

Miranda ignored him. 'Global Positioning System. It uses satellites to pinpoint your position. If you programme in the coordinates of your destination, it'll give you a route. Use it with a map and you'll never get lost. Frazer –'

'Yeah?' said Frazer, perking up.

'You get to carry the map.'

'Hmph.'

'Does it do anything else?' asked Amazon.

'Like what? You mean does it fire lasers or explode when you put it on the timer?'

Amazon blushed. She had wondered if maybe the Trackers had stuff like that.

'We're a conservation organization, Amazon, not secret agents. No, it's just GPS. Oh, and it'll tell you the time.'

While this was going on, Amazon saw that the old man, Makha, was walking around the clearing, stooping every few steps to examine the ground. He spoke to his grandson, and then to Bob Doolins. Dersu came over to the others.

'My grandfather says that Amba came back to the house last night. He says that Amba is angry, and that he must be calmed with prayers and gifts.'

At that moment Boris emerged from the cabin and barged past them. Boris the Dog followed at his heels.

'Only gift tiger get from Boris is another bullet. This time in brain. Ha ha.'

'He is a bad man,' said Dersu.

'And that is one cowardly dog,' added Amazon.

The Journey to the Boats

The river was an easy half-hour hike down through the forest from the hut. The morning was misty and cool, and the terrain almost reminded Amazon of the woods around her school. Birch, elm and hazel gave way to poplars and willows as they approached the river.

They followed a narrow track, and Boris had decided that he should be at the front. Boris the Dog would run ahead of his master for a while, putting on a show of bravery, and then would come slinking back, scared by a weasel, or a rabbit, or the falling of a leaf.

Bob Doolins was next, with his long, gangling strides eating up the forest floor. Then came the aged Makha, shuffling on his almost comically short legs. He walked with the long stick, forked at the end, which Amazon had seen him wield the night before.

After the Udege came Miranda Coverdale, her step dainty and yet forthright, her brow wrinkled in concentration. Amazon and Frazer came next,

III

walking together, with Bluey just behind them, chattering and joking. Dersu was behind Bluey, his own stride easy and fluid. An ancient rifle – as tall as the boy – was slung awkwardly over his shoulder.

At the very end came Kirov. Like Boris and Dersu, he was armed. But unlike the others he carried a Kalashnikov assault rifle.

'For defence against bandits,' he had said when challenged by Miranda.

Glancing back, Frazer found it hard not to admire the easy way he moved, and the way he looked alert without being jumpy. A good man, Frazer concluded, to have as your tail-end-Charlie on a forest trek.

His thoughts were interrupted by a bellow from Boris.

'Is river!' he yelled. 'Is boats!'

Frazer had seen many powerful rivers during his expeditions. He'd white-water rafted on the Colorado, and travelled by dugout along the Orinoco in Brazil. The Khor wasn't a frothing white-water river like the Colorado, and nor did it have the awesome majesty of the Orinoco, but it had a steady, understated power all of its own. There was none of the sort of brash, hectic energy that expresses itself in rapids and whirlpools, but rather a steady, building force, like a freight train, or lumber truck, or destiny.

It was too wide to throw a stone across, but Frazer reckoned he could skim a nice flat pebble across it in a dozen skips.

There were two boats pulled up on to the narrow shingle beach. One was a modern rigid-hulled inflatable with the TRACKS logo on the side, and a huge Yamaha 350 horsepower V8 outboard motor at the back. The other was an ancient wooden craft, scuffed and battered and patched, belonging to Makha.

'Bagsy I go in the TRACKS boat,' said Frazer, stroking the Yamaha engine.

The two Udege pushed their slender boat down into the river and stepped nimbly aboard. On a whim, Amazon joined them, although in fact there was room for everyone in the inflatable, even after all the gear was stowed. To her surprise Boris the Dog jumped in heavily after her, looking warily over his shoulder at the other Boris, who sniffed airily, as if to say 'please yourself'. It seemed that the big black dog had decided that Amazon was his new best friend.

Dersu had given the girl his hand to help her into the boat, and Makha made a little bow, and smiled a fleeting smile. It was the first smile she had seen on his weather-beaten face. He said a few words in his own native language, and then a few more in Russian.

'My grandfather welcomes you on to our boat,' said Dersu. 'But please do not fall into the river . . . it would be bad.'

Amazon wondered if this had something to do

with the strange animistic religion of the Udege. She half remembered a Russian fairy tale about water spirits, the Rusalki, who would lure young people into the water to drown them.

'Are there spirits in the water?' she asked.

Dersu looked puzzled for a moment, and then spoke to his grandfather, who smiled again, and this time the smile was full.

'Spirits?' said Dersu to Amazon. 'No. It is that we do not have the proper insurance.'

And then he pulled the cord on the old putt-putt engine and they set off, leading the much bigger inflatable into the strong current.

29

A River Cruise – and a Crash!

The river made a wonderful change after the darkness and gloom of the forest. Under the trees all Amazon had been aware of were the distant cries of birds and the occasional rustle as an invisible animal skulked away. For all she knew there were great sights around her: volcanoes, mountains, waterfalls, the ruins of lost civilizations, but in the forest all she could see were the broad trunks, the spreading branches, the dark green of the foliage.

But as soon as they hit the water, the world opened up. Suddenly there was a sky again, and the forest became a place of life and hope. In part this was simply because the curtain of foliage had been drawn back, but it was also because the edge is where things happen: life is richer at the margins between two worlds. Creatures come to the water to wash, to drink, to kill, to play.

And so Amazon gazed about with joy as the little boat puttered along. She sat on a hard bench with the muzzle of Boris the Dog on her lap, heavy as a bowling ball. Distant mountains, their peaks dipped in snow, made her feel tiny and yet somehow important at the same time. There is a special name for that feeling that mixes together pleasure and awe: the sublime, and Amazon felt it now.

Closer at hand, a golden eagle soared across the river, the feathers at the tips of its wings spread wide like fingers. Without any visible effort, it rose and perched on the naked tip of a dead pine tree.

Dersu touched her arm, pointed, and Amazon saw a wild pig drinking, with one-two-three-four-five-six stripy piglets in a line behind her. The mother looked up, stared hard with her weak eyes, grunted once, and the family trotted back into the safety of the trees.

A flash of green and gold, followed by a plop, alerted Amazon to a kingfisher, and a second after it had dived into the fast-flowing waters it emerged again, a stickleback in its dagger of a beak. She gasped at the jewelled beauty of the tiny bird, but also admired its perfection as a hunter – to the minnows the ten-centimetre kingfisher was a terrifying dragon swooping down from heaven.

'This is so beautiful,' she said to Dersu, or, rather, she said it to the world.

But it was Dersu, and not the world, who answered her.

'Yes, it is beautiful. But like all beautiful things, it

is – what is the English word . . .? The word for something that is easily broken?'

'Delicate? Fragile?'

'Yes, this is the word, *fragile*. Like the first ice of winter that even a falling leaf could break. There is pollution now in the river. The fish are not so good to eat. People come to cut down the trees. They make roads to take away the wood. Men have come to find gold. To take the gold from the earth they use chemicals that poison the river. Hunters come from the town with machine guns and kill everything, but not for food, just for the sake of killing. These are people who do not see the spirit that lives in things.'

Amazon wanted to ask more about what Dersu believed, but at that moment the inflatable, which had been keeping a set distance behind them as they cruised downstream, roared into life and shot past, sending a bow wave that almost swamped the low gunwales of the Udege boat.

'*Woo hoo!*' hollered Frazer, who was at the wheel. 'This rocks!'

Amazon thought about yelling back, that 'rocking' was exactly what you *didn't* want when you were in a boat, but it was too late – he was already out of earshot.

Frazer zigzagged for a couple of hundred metres, with Bob Doolins and Miranda Coverdale trying to wrestle control back from him, while Bluey guffawed and egged him on.

'Idiot!' said Amazon, although she couldn't stop herself from smiling.

It had been a pretty tense trip so far, and perhaps they all needed to let off steam.

And then, as she watched, the big inflatable suddenly flipped head over heels, exactly as if some giant had stuck out a foot and tripped it up. For a second she thought that this was some mad trick of Frazer's – some stunt he'd pulled off a dozen times before. And then she watched in horror as the carefully stowed gear – and, more importantly, the human cargo – flew out like the contents of a handbag held upside down and given a good shake.

30

Frazer Gets the Blame

Makha gave a guttural cry, and Dersu gunned the little engine and directed the boat to the rescue. They were at the scene in seconds.

The inflatable had been carried by an eddy into the reach of a fallen tree, so they didn't have to worry about recovering it. Miranda had made it to the same refuge, and was clinging to a branch. Boris was just tall enough to reach the bottom, and he was using his huge strength to heave himself towards the shore, holding his rifle above his head.

'Safe!' he bellowed at the Udege. 'Boris safe. You help others.'

Kirov was swimming powerfully towards Frazer, who was limp in the water. Makha skilfully steered the boat to them, and Amazon was relieved to see that Frazer's eyes were open – the spinning fall from the boat had merely dazed him.

Dersu and Amazon pulled, and Kirov pushed, and soon Frazer was in the bottom of the boat.

Amazon bent over him. 'Fraze, Fraze?'

'My baby . . .' he moaned. 'My X-Ark . . .'

Amazon tutted, and then realized that in fact the whole mission depended on the tranq guns. She scanned the choppy water, and saw that most of the baggage was snared in the same fallen tree to which Miranda was clinging. She spotted the bright aluminium case of the X-Ark.

'I think your baby's OK,' she said. 'But what happened back there?'

'There was something in the water. A deer, I think. It came out from the bank and was swimming across the river. I only saw it at the last minute. It was too late to swerve . . .'

'That's because you were going too fast.'

'Yeah, I guess so. I feel pretty stupid.'

Meanwhile Makha had directed the boat towards Doolins and Bluey. Doolins looked in a bad way. He was on his back and Bluey was trying to swim him to the shore. By the time the boat reached them Bluey had found his feet, and together they all got Doolins up on to the muddy bank. He had a cut over one eye, and his right arm hung limp at his side.

Miranda Coverdale swung into action, despite her own scratches and bruises. She was a trained vet, rather than a doctor, but as she said: 'When it comes to treating wounds, there's no difference between a pig and a person.'

'Can someone get my pack?' she said as she examined Doolins. 'It's caught in the tree. My medical kit is inside.'

Amazon went back into the river and edged along the fallen tree until the water was up to her chest. The water was ice cold – it had, after all, flowed down from the high mountains. The current forced her into the network of branches, which poked and scratched at her as if they deliberately wanted to do her damage. But she reached Miranda's pack and hooked it over her arm.

'Good work,' said Miranda. She didn't give much in the way of praise, and Amazon felt a surge of pride.

Soon Miranda had Doolins's head bandaged, while the others recovered what they could from the disaster.

As well as the gear caught in the fallen tree, some pieces of equipment had washed up further downstream, and other items were stranded on a shingle bank in the middle of the river. Kirov took charge of the operation, and even Boris went to work without complaining.

The biggest problem was that the satellite communications equipment was all either lost or destroyed.

Frazer and Amazon were given the job of lighting a fire. Frazer was unusually quiet, and Amazon sensed that he was really upset about having caused the accident. She took pity on him.

'Sure,' she said, 'you were going too fast, but it wasn't your fault that the deer came out in front of you. It could have happened to anyone. I suppose.'

Frazer nodded back to her.

'Thanks. I may be an idiot sometimes, but I only ever make a mistake once. Next time I'll swerve.'

Amazon tried not to, but in the end she couldn't help but smile, although she accompanied it with an eye-roll and a friendly tut.

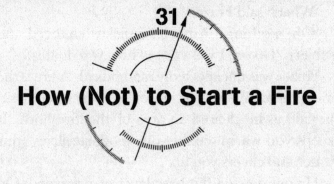

31

How (Not) to Start a Fire

Frazer and Amazon collected some dry wood for the fire from the edge of the forest. Although they were too embarrassed to say anything out loud, they both had that feeling that something was lurking in there, not very far away, watching them. It made them hurry back to the others.

'How are we going to light it?' asked Amazon, looking down at the sticks.

'Watch and learn,' replied Frazer, who was almost back to his old self. 'I've started fires pretty well everywhere in my time. My dad showed me. He was the best.'

Amazon remembered something her own father had told her, years before. He didn't speak much about his brother, Hal, but he had said that there were two things that his brother was good at making: wind and fire. And sometimes he linked the two together. The memory made her splutter with laughter.

'What?' said Frazer.

'Oh, nothing.' Amazon quickly changed the subject. 'Go on, I want to see how you do this.'

Frazer was unexpectedly methodical. 'A fire is the most important thing when you're in the wilderness,' he said as he cleared an area of the foreshore. 'It keeps you warm, cooks your food, sterilizes your water and cheers you up.'

He put down a flat base layer of dry wood. On top of that he put a layer of silvery bark, stripped from a rotten log.

'Birch bark has flammable oils in it,' he explained as he worked. 'Burns like a dream.'

On top of the bark he placed two bundles of small twigs, crossed over each other. Then he prepared a pile of larger sticks by the side.

He peeled another piece of bark off the rotten log, and used the small blade on his multi-tool to shave and scrape and score at the pale inner surface, giving it a feathery appearance.

'Now for the fun bit,' he said, digging down into the zippered pocket of his combat trousers.

Amazon assumed he had some matches in there, and she was going to say that they'd be useless because of the soaking they'd all got. But what Frazer finally pulled out – after a ball of string, some loose change and a clump of sodden tissues – was not a box of matches. It was a piece of metal, about half the size of a pencil.

'What's that?'

'It's a firesteel.'

'A what?'

'It's a special metal alloy. Just watch.'

He then lined up the piece of metal with the feathered bark and scraped the multi-tool blade along its length. It produced a gratifying shower of sparks, which fizzed on to the bark. It was like a miniature firework display. Amazon let out an involuntary little gasp.

Unfortunately, despite Frazer's gentle blowing, the first set of sparks didn't quite take hold. Frazer got ready to try again. Amazon was sure it would work this time.

However Frazer didn't get a second chance. The two children were so engrossed in what they were doing they didn't notice that others had gathered round to watch. Now Boris barged forward and roughly shoved Frazer aside.

'Hey!' yelped Frazer.

'This take too long. If we wait for you, winter will be here and all will freeze, eh? Boris show you how Russian man make a fire – not like stupid Yankee.'

And then Boris pulled the clip from his hunting rifle – actually a World War Two, Mosin-Nagant sniper rifle – and snapped out a bullet. He twisted the cartridge open, and emptied out the black powder at the base of the neat woodpile Amazon and Frazer had built. Then he shoved the clip back in the rifle.

'Back!' he said, and fired a bullet into the little pyramid of black powder.

This all happened so quickly that no one had time to react. But now pandemonium broke out. Simultaneously the powder burst into flame, wood scattered and splintered, Frazer and Amazon dived for cover, and Kirov charged into Boris, cursing him so violently in Russian that the words seemed like axe blows.

It looked as if the two men were going to fight it out to the death, and Frazer's money would be on the smaller man. His eyes burned like sapphire lasers.

But the fight never happened. Boris looked down and then away, and then muttered to himself.

'Fire is lit,' he said sulkily, and so it was.

32

The Journey Resumes

Soon they were all warm and dry. Makha and Dersu had found the body of the deer that had caused the accident floating in the water. It was of the species known in Russia as the izyubr – a close relative of the European red deer and North American elk.

This was a magnificent specimen, with antlers as wide as Boris's outspread arms. The two Udege quickly skinned and butchered the carcass, and soon skewers of venison were cooking on the fire.

However it was not a happy group.

Doolins was agitated about the time they'd lost, and there was bad blood among the rest of the group, most of it centred on Boris, who'd managed to fall out with pretty well everyone there.

'How far is it to the area of the forest fire?' Miranda asked Doolins.

'Another hour and we should be at the site,' he said. 'Let's just hope we make it before the fire is totally out of control.' He turned to Frazer, who was trying to keep a low profile. 'I hope you've learned your lesson here, boy. Someone could have been killed. And we've lost some of the fire-fighting equipment the troops needed.'

Surprisingly it was Kirov who spoke up for him.

'The boy was not really to blame. That deer came out of the forest very fast. And when he swam in the water, only his head was showing. Not easy for the boy to see.'

Dersu suddenly was paying very close attention. He spoke to his grandfather, who replied in a tone of great agitation.

'This is bad sign,' Dersu said. 'Izyubr is only afraid of one thing: Amba!'

At the word 'Amba' Boris the Dog whined and snuggled close to Amazon. She stroked his ears. She was growing fond of the stupid, cowardly creature. 'It must be the same tiger that was at the cabin last night,' Dersu continued. 'My grandfather is unhappy. We must go.'

In half an hour they were back on the water.

Frazer had asked Dersu if he could ride in their boat. 'Bit awkward over in the inflatable,' he'd said.

'Of course,' said Dersu. 'But my grandfather thinks it best if I am at the helm. We have killed enough deer for one day.'

It wasn't much later that Amazon caught the first whiff of smoke, and soon Frazer was pointing out the angry grey plume lying over the land ahead on the right shore of the river.

In a few more minutes they came upon a ragged collection of tents by the river. Beyond them the forest was engulfed in thick smoke, pierced here and there by flashes of intense red flame. The boats pulled in, and a group of Russian soldiers appeared. Most of them had cigarettes in their mouths, which struck Amazon as pretty stupid given the situation.

'Looks like Mr Doolins has his work cut out with that lot,' said Frazer.

'Not good men,' added Dersu. 'Not good men at all.'

33

Amba, Again

After he had left the clearing, driven away by that strange smell and the feeling of 'badness' that emanated from the cabin, Amba had followed the track down to the river. From there he had moved quickly, following the river's course.

He was still determined to destroy his spotted rival. But that didn't mean he wasn't peckish.

And so when he saw the izyubr he decided that vengeance could wait a little while.

He stalked the big deer, creeping forward to within pouncing distance. With smaller prey – a wild pig or the graceful roe deer – Amba would leap on the animal's back, and bite through the vertebrae of the neck, bringing a swift death.

However, with prey as large as a full-grown izyubr, Amba's technique was to attack from behind, and then to come up almost beneath the victim so as to get a grip on the throat. Death was just as sure, but much slower as the animal suffocated.

Now, just as Amba was ready to take the three bounding strides towards the izyubr, the wind changed direction, and his strong feline stink reached the deer. Instantly the stag's head was up, and his senses – hearing and sight as well as smell – fired into life. Amba charged, but the izyubr was already bounding away. The tiger followed. All was not lost. The deer was heading towards the river and Amba could outswim any deer.

The terrified izyubr burst from the trees and splashed out into the water. Amba was about to close on his victim, and then he saw the boats, and recognized his enemy of the previous night – the small ancient human who should have feared him and yet did not.

Amba stopped, growled and retreated. The deer, still convinced that the predator was about to sink its teeth and claws into his flanks, carried on.

Right into the path of the onrushing inflatable.

Thwarted again, Amba continued on his way, more determined than ever now to find and kill the leopard and her cubs.

34

The Party Splits Up

The smoke made the air acrid and bitter, and stung Amazon's eyes, as Doolins, his head bandaged and his arm in a sling, gave them their final instructions.

'So, as agreed with Ms Coverdale, the three teams are: one, Amazon and Frazer with Dersu and Makha; two, Miranda with Boris; and, three, Bluey and Kirov. Team one, you'll take the side nearest the Khor River. Team two, you'll trek across to the Ussuri River, and work your way down from there. Team three, you go down the middle. Each team will have a tranq rifle. And you've each got a receiver to pick up the signal from the radio collar. As you know, we lost the sat phones in the, er, *accident* . . .' Doolins paused, but didn't look at Frazer, for which the boy was very grateful. 'And there's no chance of a normal mobile signal in these mountains. What this means is that we must have a fixed rendezvous at the point where the two rivers meet. That's about sixteen miles from the drop-off.

'It's fifteen hundred hours now. Twenty-four hours should be enough for you to work your way from here to there. So I'll be waiting with the inflatable at this time tomorrow. I suggest you set the timers on those fancy watches of yours.'

Amazon clicked through to the stopwatch function on her GPS watch, and set it to twenty-four hours.

'I don't need to tell you to be careful,' Doolins continued. 'Leopards are dangerous animals – none more so than a mother defending her cubs. And we don't know if there's a tiger in there as well, but there may be. And there are reports of hunters. And topping it all off is the fire – if the wind strengthens, then it could trap you. I'll do what I can with the soldiers here to construct a firebreak, but realistically it's down to you to find and rescue the leopards. Remember, if you fail, and the leopards don't make it, then this whole conservation project will be closed down, and the local government will sell the land off to loggers. Any questions? No? Good. See you in twenty-four hours.'

A scruffy and sulky Russian soldier ferried the three parties around the burning line of fire in the inflatable. They unloaded their gear and the boat zoomed away.

'This is where we part, then,' said Miranda. 'Frazer, I'm counting on you to take good care of Amazon. Trust your guides and do what they say. Take no risks.

The leopard is important, but people are more important still. Got that?'

'Sure,' said Frazer, although he wasn't really listening. He felt that at last the adventure was really beginning.

'Take it easy, kid,' said Bluey, ruffling Amazon's hair. 'Don't let the boy genius here get into any trouble.'

Boris the Dog came to say goodbye. He snuffled at Amazon's feet and whined and slobbered. Amazon reached into her pack and found a small piece of chocolate.

'Take this you silly thing,' she said, and he snaffled it up.

Then Boris the man came and dragged him away, saying, 'Give candy to dog is bad. Make dog lazy. Lazy dog is as much use as gun without bullet.'

'Small treats are OK, sometimes, for dogs and for people,' said Amazon.

'Perhaps,' said Boris, shrugging. 'But let me give advice to English girl. Is old Russian saying, *Ot dobra dobra ne ishchut*.'

'And that means?'

'It means, English girl, be careful.'

And then Boris spat on the forest floor, and walked away, Boris the Dog slinking at his heels.

Bluey and Miranda gave a final wave, and Kirov saluted before following after the big Russian and his dog, leaving Amazon and Frazer with Dersu and Makha.

But the parting wasn't yet quite over. After about a hundred metres, Boris the Dog paused and looked back over his shoulder at Amazon. His master stopped also, and spoke roughly to him. The dog looked from Boris to Amazon and back again. Boris shouted and then he aimed a kick at his dog. It wasn't an especially vicious kick, but it was the final straw. Boris the Dog lifted a back leg and let out a disdainful stream of water in the general direction of his master, and then ran back to the other group. He jumped up and put his heavy paws on Amazon's shoulders and licked her face.

'Keep stupid lazy coward dog!' yelled Boris with a dismissive wave of his hand. 'Good only as food for tiger.'

And then he turned and went on his way, muttering in Russian.

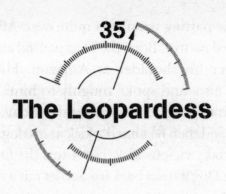

35

The Leopardess

She had found what seemed like a safe new den for her cubs: a burrow dug out by a fox or jackal under the spreading roots of a big larch tree. And the hunting was suddenly spectacular: she had never seen so many of the beautiful spotted sika deer, or big izyubr, or the goat-like antelope called the goral. She wasn't to know that they were all bottled up by the fire.

It was a sika deer she was eating now, beginning, as leopards always do, with the hindquarters. And as she ate, her cubs suckled, batting at each other with paws that were not yet the lethal killing machines they would one day become.

One of her cubs – the youngest and cheekiest – crawled on to her back, digging his sharp little claws through her fur and into her skin. He reached the plastic collar round her neck – it was so light that the leopardess had forgotten it was there. But the cub took exception to this thing that was so obviously not supposed to be part of his mother. He chewed and worried at it. But the radio transmitter was designed to take that sort of punishment, and soon the cub got bored, and rolled off her back. Time to tease his sister.

Despite the safe den and fine hunting, which meant that her cubs were growing fat on her rich milk, the leopardess was still uneasy. It wasn't just the smell of distant smoke. It was the knowledge that her only natural enemies, the tiger and man, were here. She pulled the complaining cubs close to her and wrapped herself protectively around them.

36

Into the Forest's Heart

'OK,' said Frazer, unpacking the radio receiver. 'Let's track this baby down!'

The receiver part of the tracking equipment consisted of a small hand-held device, a little bigger than a mobile phone, with a large fold-out antenna like a portable TV aerial. The handset had an on/off switch, and a line of LED lights to indicate the signal strength. Frazer flicked the 'on' button, and held the device up.

'It should beep if the leopard is anywhere within a couple of miles,' he said.

Dersu and Makha exchanged looks, their faces interested, but ever so slightly amused. This was definitely not the Udege way of tracking.

Frazer waited for the beep that would tell him that their quarry was near.

Silence. And not a flicker from the LEDs.

'Nothing. It must be out of range. Guess it's down to you guys for a while,' he said to Dersu.

Makha was already walking, the long forked stick in his gnarled hand, picking his way carefully into the forest. Frazer, still clutching the (so far) useless tracking device, looked at Amazon, and gave her an encouraging nod. Then they followed the leader, Amazon struggling under her heavy pack, but still amazed and delighted to be in such an unexpected place. She felt oddly comforted by the presence of Boris the Dog at her heels – proven coward though he be. Dersu, as watchful as ever, brought up the rear.

Soon they were deep in the heart of the forest. The only sounds were the soft *clump* of their feet in the leaf litter and Boris the Dog's heavy panting.

Makha was still in the lead. His head was bowed as he studied the ground intently. Then he stopped dead, and crouched a little stiffly. The others bunched up behind him.

'Has your grandfather found the tracks of the leopard?' asked Frazer, his voice bubbling with suppressed excitement.

'Possibly.'

Frazer looked disappointed. 'Only possibly? I thought you guys could track anything.'

'I will explain,' Dersu replied patiently. 'This path is made by the wild pigs. And where pigs go the leopard will go too. In winter, to follow an animal is easy, because of the snow. Even a spirit as wise as the leopard or the tiger does not think about the footprints it leaves. My grandfather does not understand this blindness to such a thing, but it is so. It means that in the snow you can tell everything. You can see where the leopard has walked, where it has rested, where it has rolled to one side to give milk to its babies, where it has waited in hiding for its dinner to walk by. How many steps it took before the leap that killed the izyubr. All these things my grandfather can read in the snow. But this is no great skill. Even a stupid Russian from the city like that idiot Boris can follow a leopard or a tiger in the snow, and shoot it with a machine gun.'

'But now there is no snow . . .'

'Of course, and now, at the end of the summer, is the most difficult time to track. Not only is there no snow, but the ground is hard and dry. The trail is like the trail of a ghost. Boris could not follow. Even I could not follow, and I have learnt much from my grandfather. But yes, my grandfather will find the trail. He is the greatest tracker living among our people, and our people are the greatest trackers in the world.'

Dersu's words were so unlike the boasting of Boris. They were spoken in a matter-of-fact way, as if he was telling you the time or pointing out the name of a tree.

'I hate to tell you, Dersu,' said Frazer, 'but –' he

was about to say that almost every group of indigenous people he'd met, from Australia to South America, reckoned they were the best trackers in the world, but at that moment Makha grunted and climbed back to his feet. He said a few words to Dersu.

'He has found the signs. We chase the leopard, and the leopard chases the sika,' said Dersu, translating. 'And when she catches her prey, we will catch ours.'

37

I'm Still Falling

The excitement that Amazon and Frazer felt on finally being on the trail of the leopard lasted for as long as it took them to make the first long, hard climb up the side of one of the many hills that rose and rippled in the land between the two rivers.

So far all the trekking they had done had been fairly easy, on level ground along established tracks. But this was very different. Once they were away from the riverbank there was no level ground at all. They were either heaving themselves up hills or carefully picking their way down. And in between each of the hills the land was damp and boggy, with usually a stream to negotiate – which often meant wet boots to add to the lack of comfort.

Amazon had never walked with such a heavy pack before, and her legs ached as she pushed herself up the slopes. However, she almost preferred the going up to the going down. The problem was that she was worried the pack would make her fall forward flat on her face – which was something she particularly wanted to avoid. Therefore she overcompensated, leant back and twice overbalanced backwards.

The first time was embarrassing and undignified. She let out a squeal and slithered a metre or so over the loose leaf litter and then rolled to a halt. Frazer gave her a hand up, and was about to make one of his jokes, but then saw her face and wisely decided against it.

The second time was very different, and much more dangerous. They had just slogged to the top of one of the rises. It was late afternoon by now and Amazon was exhausted. Her legs felt like they'd been taken away and surgically replaced by a substance more like marshmallow.

At the very top of the hill there were no trees at all, just low bushes and a tussocky grass as rough and tough as sandpaper. At the top Amazon paused to take in the view, but the others pushed on back down again.

Amazon increased her pace to catch up, and suddenly she was on her back and sliding. She didn't have time to cry out before she careered into Frazer who, in turn, bashed into Dersu. The three of them were sliding down on the loose leaves, with Boris the Dog barking along excitedly, and only Makha left to save them from a steep and possibly fatal fall.

He turned, looked at them in a puzzled way, as if to say 'What are these young people up to now?' and then jabbed his staff into the ground at an angle across the line of their descent.

Dersu, Amazon and Frazer crashed into the stick.

Amazon thought that there was no way such a frail-looking old man could hold them all, but he planted his stout legs, grunted and they were saved.

Makha then calmly walked on again, without a word.

Falling together in a heap is one good way of cementing a friendship, and suddenly Frazer and Amazon felt closer to Dersu, especially as he did not seem to mind being bowled over by them. He smiled and helped them up.

'I remember a Russian joke that I heard when I was at school in Moscow,' he said. 'Two men are walking in the woods, when one falls down an old well. The other runs over and calls down into the black hole. "My friend," he yells, "can you hear me? Are you OK?" "Yes," says the friend, "I can hear you." "Are you badly hurt? Have you broken any bones?" "No, am not badly hurt, and I don't think I've broken any bones." "Thank goodness. And what is it like at the bottom of the well?" "I don't know," says the friend. "I'm still falling."'

It took a moment or two for Amazon and Frazer to get the joke, but then they all laughed together, and once again trudged after Makha.

38

The Travellers' Rest

At the top of the next rise they had a much-needed rest. They unshouldered their packs and found rocks to sit on. Boris the Dog curled himself into an untidy heap and went straight to sleep.

The view before Amazon was truly spectacular. It was late summer now, and the first leaves were beginning to turn golden, emphasized by the touch of the sun, sinking ever lower in the sky.

'Amazing, isn't it?' said Frazer, squatting next to Amazon. 'I did tons of background reading on it. Out here you get three different forests for your money. Low down in the valley bottoms you get the sort of trees that like it wet and marshy – you see way down there, those tall skinny poplars and drooping willows?'

'Uh-huh,' said Amazon, too tired to take it in. It didn't stop Frazer from carrying on with his mini lecture.

'A little higher up the slopes and you come to what

is known as the Manchurian broadleaf forest. There are maples, birches and elms just like the ones we get in Europe and America, but there are also Manchurian ash, Mongolian oak, the Amur cork tree and other unique species.'

'Uh-huh.'

'And there you can see, the next layer up is dominated by evergreen pine and fir and spruce. The Russians call this the dark-coniferous taiga. It is the sort of forest that covers almost the whole of Siberia to the north, and it is the realm of hunters like the brown bear and the wolf.'

'Uh-huh.'

'And then at the top, where we are now, it's too high for trees, so you just get this tussocky alpine grassland –'

'Uh-huh.'

If Amazon had been less tired she would have enjoyed both the lecture and the wonderful view across the seemingly endless forest, rolling away beneath them like a green sea.

The only thing ruining it was the dark line of smoke and the dull red glow coming from the fires away to the east.

'May as well try this thing again,' said Frazer, setting up the radio receiver.

He held the aerial high above his head and slowly turned round.

'Still nothing,' he groaned.

'Could the transmitter thingy on the leopard be faulty?' asked Amazon, pulling the water bottle from her pack and taking a gulp.

'They're pretty reliable. It's more likely that the terrain is getting in the way. Radio waves can't go through rock.'

Dersu approached them in his usual humble and courteous way.

'My grandfather says we must hurry. It is almost time to make a camp for the night.'

And so they began to march down again, still following the trails made by wild pigs, along which the stealthy leopard had also walked.

Now she was back in the middle of it, rather than enjoying it from above, Amazon couldn't help but feel a little disappointed in the forest. Most of what she knew about such places she'd learnt from TV documentaries, and that had led her to expect that the forest would be full of life and colour.

Of course she knew that she wouldn't be seeing monkeys swinging through the trees or birds of paradise displaying in the branches. But apart from the darkly silent trees, the only living things here seemed to be huge ugly mosquitoes, and horseflies, and the tiny even more annoying gnats. And now that the day was waning the mosquitoes were worse than ever.

She stopped, and dug down in her pack for the insect repellent.

Frazer saw what she was doing and called ahead for the guides to wait.

'Those no-see-ums are a pest, ain't they?' he said in his usual friendly and open way. 'But at least there don't seem to be any leeches yet. I once had one as big as a snake fastened on to my neck. And I didn't even feel it, because they inject you with an anaesthetic . . .'

Amazon had a particular hatred for even the thought of leeches, and she quickly changed the subject, when suddenly she saw something – a flash of deep golden fur in the undergrowth a few metres behind Frazer.

And there!

Another glimpse of the same beautiful, burning, deadly colour.

This thing was big – at least two metres long. There was only one golden creature of that size in these forests.

Straight away Amazon thought: *Cripes*, we *were looking for the leopard, but the tiger has found* us.

39

The Biggest Weasels
in the World

Frazer realized that Amazon wasn't looking at him, and that her face was rigid with fear. He turned slowly and saw the object of her gaze. And, like her, he immediately thought *big cat*.

He began to back away. And then he stopped, and smiled.

'What is it?' hissed Amazon.

Frazer put his hand on her shoulder and whispered in her ear. 'It's fine – look closely.'

And as she looked, Amazon realized that what she was looking at wasn't one large predator, but two smaller ones.

'Small', however, is a relative term. These were the biggest – and most beautiful – weasels Amazon had ever seen. Their bodies were a rich gold, and their legs and tails a lovely nut brown. They were the size of foxes, but had the busy, predatory energy of all the weasel family.

'They're yellow-throated martens,' he whispered.

'What? How do you know?'

'Hey, mammals of the world – it's my thing!'

'Oh. Are they dangerous?' asked Amazon.

It was an odd question to be directed at something the length of her arm, but the martens looked utterly fearless.

'They can be. Packs of them have been known to attack humans.'

'Are you winding me up?'

'Not this time. But these two look like they're after easier pickings than us, Zonnie.'

And it was clear even to Amazon that the martens were on the trail of something. Their long necks twisted and writhed as they sniffed at the ground, darting back and forth. Then they were off.

At the same moment, Boris the Dog appeared at Amazon's side. He had also caught a glimpse of the martens, but had waited until they were heading safely in the opposite direction before he decided to make his presence felt. Now he managed a single gruff bark.

Dersu and Makha had followed the dog back.

'Yellow-throated martens,' said Frazer eagerly. 'I think they've scented something.'

Dersu passed this on to Makha. They consulted for a few seconds.

'We must follow,' said Dersu. 'It is possible that martens have found the scent of leopard kill. But not dog – will scare leopard.'

Amazon looked at Boris. She didn't want to tie him up – not with all those predators around.

'Right, Boris the Dog, you listen, and listen good. You can't come with us, so you'll have to stay right here. You get that? Stay!'

Boris looked at her, drooled and wagged his tail.

'Dersu, how do you say "stay" in Russian?'

Dersu shrugged. '*Os-tay-sya.*'

'*Os-tay-sya!*' said Amazon in a strict voice.

To her amazement, Boris the Dog lay down on the ground, resting his slobbery muzzle on his front paws.

'Hey, you *are* good with animals,' said Frazer. 'But if we're going to catch up with those weasels . . .'

And with that the four of them set off in hot pursuit of the golden hunters.

For the first time they were away from the trail and amid the full tangled glory of the forest. Thorns tore at their clothing, briars and brambles tangled around them and roots tripped them. It seemed to Amazon that there was no way they could follow such swift and elusive creatures, moving as they did like sunlight through the forest, but every so often they would catch a reassuring glimpse of gold through the green, and know that they were still in with a chance.

After fifteen breathless minutes, Makha slowed and then crouched down behind the massive, moss-covered trunk of a fallen tree. Amazon, who was at his shoulder, realized that for the first time the old man was out of breath. But there, in a small clearing, was their quarry.

40

At the Kill

Frazer had seen plenty of kills in his time, so he knew what to expect. Amazon, however, had never seen a death like this before, red and gory and flecked with black flies.

And then there was the smell – disgusting, but somehow sweet, like rotten fruit.

She was repelled. And upset. But also fascinated. And deep down she knew that if she were to become a real Tracker, someone who would contribute to the vital work of saving animals around the planet, this was exactly the kind of thing to which she had to get used. So she gritted her teeth, and tied her mother's spotted neckerchief round her nose and mouth.

The kill was a female sika deer. The doe's beautiful spotted coat – what was left of it – was dappled by the late-afternoon light. Amazon could clearly see the bloody marks where the teeth had clamped round the lovely, slender neck, and slowly choked the life out of it.

Much of the back end of the carcass had already been eaten, and it was there that the two yellow-throated martens were making merry, burrowing into the raw red flesh with busy, silent intensity.

Dersu whispered in her ear: 'This is the leopard's kill. You see, the leopard always begins to eat from here.' At this Dersu patted his backside. 'It will return to eat again. Then you will have your chance to shoot with your toy gun.'

Frazer was already opening the X-Ark case.

'This ain't no toy, my friend,' he said without any bitterness.

Frazer carefully loaded one of the darts, slotting it into the chamber, accessed through the stock at the back of the gun. Then he stroked the X-Ark a couple of times, the way you would a puppy, and handed it to Amazon.

She looked at him in amazement.

'Truth is, Zonnie, I can't shoot straight to save my life. And this might be our only chance.'

She was going to argue back, saying that it was Frazer's gun, but in their hearts they both knew that what he said was true, and that the needs of the mission came first. She squeezed his arm, and took the X-Ark.

Frazer at least had his camera.

'Not many people have photographed the Amur leopard at a kill,' he said, holding up the expensive device. 'Might be able to sell some shots to *National Geographic*.'

Amazon checked the sights on the X-Ark. She aimed at the deer and flicked the laser quickly on and off – even so it seemed to be enough to startle the martens, who pulled their heads out of the deer's haunch and looked around, craning their long necks.

And then Amazon realized that it wasn't the laser light that had startled them – how could it be when they were halfway inside the deer?

Something was coming.

'Get ready,' said Frazer, which slightly annoyed Amazon.

'Of course I'm getting ready,' she hissed back through the neckerchief. 'What do you think I'm doing, polishing my nails?'

She gazed into the dense undergrowth. There was a sound, a rustling. But there was something wrong. The sound was coming from above them. She looked up. Yes, there was a shadow there, pushing through the leaves.

Of course, thought Amazon, *the leopard might well arrive through the branches*. Leopards were superb climbers, weren't they?

But something about the big, dark shape in the tree didn't really seem, well, leopard-like. It was too clumsy.

Too noisy.

Too black.

It looked more like a gorilla or a . . .

'Bear,' said Dersu. 'Black bear.'

'Gee,' said Frazer, 'I know black bears can climb, but in America they don't usually get around like that, in the treetops, like chimps . . .'

'Here the bear is afraid of the tiger, and so he spends nearly all of his time in the tree,' said Dersu.

By this time the bear was shinning awkwardly backwards down the trunk, looking like a fat man in a fur coat.

With a final jump – which was, in truth, more like a fall – he landed not very far from the deer.

'Oh, that's so cool,' said Frazer. 'It's an Asiatic black bear – you can identify it by the white bib at its throat.'

'Is it dangerous?' Amazon asked yet again, thinking of what Frazer had said about the much smaller martens. In truth, the creature in the clearing almost looked friendly.

'They're usually harmless enough, as long as you don't get in between a mom and her cubs. Or unless they're very, *very* hungry . . .'

As they watched, the bear – a rather scruffy-looking old boy, shuffled towards the deer carcass.

The two yellow-throated martens chittered and showed their teeth, but they were no match for the bear. In any case, they had eaten their fill. They flowed away though the undergrowth, as fluid and graceful as ever, despite their bellies full of venison.

Now it was the old bear's turn to settle down to

its dinner. It shoved its head into the deer with a noise like a toothless old man slurping soup.

Makha had been enjoying the show as much as the children, but suddenly his expression changed from concentrated interest in what was happening out in the clearing to puzzlement; and then something close to dismay. Dersu was about to speak to him, but the trapper clamped his hand over the boy's mouth.

41

The Brown Giant

Amazon and Frazer looked at him in surprise, but before they had the chance to ask what was going on they found out for themselves, for there, lumbering out into the clearing, they saw a shaggy giant.

Amazon was no expert on bears, but she knew that this was a very different proposition to the scruffy old black bear, with its look of baffled dignity. This new arrival was simply immense, with a great hump of muscle swelling up between its shoulder blades. Each paw seemed like a huge war-club, complete with the long curving claws, like blades. The bear carried its head low to the ground, which added to the air of menace.

This was one of the famous and fearsome Ussuri brown bears – a close cousin of the grizzly, but with an even more fearsome reputation. It had smelled the meat, and it was coming to collect. It spotted the black impostor, gave a mighty bellow and charged.

The charge was in the direction of the fallen tree

behind which Amazon, Frazer, Makha and Dersu were hiding. It was impossible for Amazon and Frazer not to flinch – but even the wise old trapper and his grandson cowered further down behind the tree.

So busy was the old black bear at its feast that the first it knew about its rival was when one of those huge paws swept it aside as easily as you'd brush a fly from your dinner plate. The black bear uttered not a sound, but hurried away, dragging its injured back leg. It was heading straight for the concealed humans.

There was no knowing what might happen next. The black bear might be sulky and decide to take out its disappointment on them. It might strike out with its impressive claws as it passed.

Even worse, it might in some way draw the attention of the brown giant to their hiding place. But at the last second the black bear remembered that adult brown bears are too heavy to climb, and so its best hope of safety lay up in the trees.

Huffing and grunting, the black bear scuttled with surprising speed up into the protecting branches of a Korean pine, and made its escape high above the ground.

The brown bear stood on its back legs to survey the clearing. It towered more than three metres high, a grim brown ogre.

Makha pulled at Dersu.

'We go now,' said Dersu.

Amazon took no convincing. The black bear had amused and intrigued her, but she was trembling at the sight of the brown bear.

Frazer, however, was determined to get his shot. He focused his lens on the bear as it moved slowly to the deer carcass and clicked.

Instantly, the bear stopped. Frazer heard Makha hiss. He watched the bear's ears swivel, like radar dishes. Makha signalled that they stay perfectly still. Any sound and the bear would come over to investigate, and if that happened then not all of them would live.

A more nervous bear might well have checked out the clearing a little more thoroughly, but this was the biggest bear in the whole of the Russian Far East. Nothing scared it – and it was hungry. So, with one big, huffing snort, it settled down next to the deer and started to eat.

'Now we go,' said Dersu. And they left, creeping away like assassins.

42

The Camp

'We must get as far away as possible before we make our camp,' said Dersu when they had put enough distance between themselves and the bear to be out of earshot. Makhu looked genuinely distressed, which seemed a little odd to Amazon, given the way he had faced down the tiger the night before.

'I second that,' said Frazer. 'That was the biggest bear I've ever seen.'

'My people fear the bear more than Amba,' said Dersu. 'The tiger here is not like the tiger in India. They are very seldom man-eaters. They attack when they are hunted or injured – never do they choose to kill people for food. But the bear is different. He is clever and he eats whatever he wants. And sometimes what he wants is man.'

Makha soon found the forest trail. They picked up Boris the Dog, who was fast asleep in the exact spot they had left him, and after half an hour of forced marching they reached a flat area near the river that satisfied the old tracker's strict requirements for a campsite.

Makha and Dersu slung down their packs and then disappeared, Dersu carrying a hatchet. While they were gone Frazer and Amazon prepared the fire. Frazer let Amazon have a go at lighting it with his firesteel. It was actually pretty easy, Amazon found, as long as you had good dry tinder.

Soon Dersu and Makha returned carrying great armfuls of spruce branches and some long trimmed poles. In ten minutes they had constructed a lean-to, open on one side, with a roof of fir, and with more fir piled on the floor to form a thick, springy mattress.

Amazon looked at Frazer. 'I hadn't really thought about where we're going to sleep. Should we make one of those things too?'

'Well, that would be kind of fun, I guess. Except for the bugs.'

Dusk was the prime hunting time for bloodsuckers, and big clouds of mosquitoes and gnats had found them. Despite the insect repellent, Amazon could already feel the bites beginning to itch.

'And of course,' Frazer continued, a half-smile on his face, 'if that old bear happens by, and sees you lying there, he might just decide on a snack . . .'

'THAT'S NOT FUNNY, FRAZER! I can't believe you let me come out here without a tent . . .'

'Well, that would have been dumb of me, wouldn't it?'

And then Frazer reached into his pack and pulled out a thin disc of material. With a quick flip, it pinged open, and where two seconds before there had been nothing but bare earth, now there was a neat little tent.

'Very clever,' said Amazon. 'And where's mine?'

'Hate to tell you, Zonnie, but that's a two-guy tent.'

'No way!'

'Way. Unless you want to spend the night out with the bugs and the bears . . .?'

Amazon groaned, but didn't argue.

Half an hour later the four of them were gathered around the campfire, eating a stew of beans and rice which, to Amazon's relief, didn't taste of anything much.

Makha had been staring into the fire while the young people chatted. Now he began to speak, and it seemed to Amazon that he spoke not to them, but to the fire. Dersu translated but, mysteriously, the voices blended together, so that it felt to Amazon and to Frazer that there was only one speaker, and that was the old man.

The Story of the Killer Bear

'Sixty years ago when I was a boy, there were still Korean villages in the valleys. You could tell that they were Korean because they were clean and neat and the houses were all painted white.

'In one of these villages I had a friend, called Dorea. We used to play together while my father sold wild ginseng to the Koreans. This is why I knew of the people and the village, and the terrible events that occurred. Dorea was my special friend, although her people did not want for her to play with a "savage" like me.

'Anyway, it was at the end of the winter. A family in the Korean village was sitting down to dinner, when they thought there was a knocking at the door. The man, whose name was Shin, sent his wife to see who was there. He heard a scream, and saw the woman being carried away by a bear.

'He ran to get his gun and chased the bear into the forest. He followed the tracks and the blood in the snow for two hours. He found the bear and fired, but his gun was old and exploded and knocked him out. When he woke up he saw that there were bear tracks all around where he lay. He did not understand why the bear had not killed him.

'When he got back to his home he found that the bear had returned before him and killed his two children. He knew then that the bear was evil and had left him alive so he could see his children had been killed.

'The village spent the next week in mourning for the dead. On the last night of mourning the bear returned to the village. It broke down the door of a house. Inside the house there were two women. The women fought the bear with pots and pans and knives and everything they could find, but the bear mortally hurt one woman, who told the story of what happened before she died, and took away the other woman into the forest.

'Now the headman of the village went to the town to ask for help. The chief of police told him he would send men soon. On his way back to the village the headman was killed and eaten by the bear. At least that is what was said. Nothing was ever found of him and he may just have run away because of shame or fear.

'The police finally came, but not for a week, and by then the bear had killed a boy who was playing in front of his house. His mother had told him not to go out, but the boy became bored, as boys will.

'Five policemen went to track the bear. Many of the villagers went with them, some armed with guns, others carrying pitchforks and scythes. One even had a sword from the days of his ancestors. When they were out in the forest, the bear returned for the last time to the village and killed a blind man, and also the girl, Dorea, who was my friend.

'The policemen came back from the forest and saw what had happened and then they ran away, saying that the bear was indeed a demon, and could not be killed.

'It was then that my father and I returned to the village. We had been deep in the forest gathering ginseng, and knew nothing of the bear. I wept when I heard that my friend Dorea had been killed. I remember that my father scolded me for acting like a child. Then he spoke to the man, Shin, and together we three went into the forest. My father tracked the bear back to a cave. At the mouth of the cave there were many bones, the bones of deer and moose and even the bones of a tiger, as well as the bones of some of the people the bear had killed.

'My father set alight the brush at the mouth of the cave. He gave his good rifle to the man Shin, and when the smoke forced the bear from the cave, Shin shot the bear.

'But the bear was not killed, although the bullet

entered his chest. The bear was enraged and killed the man Shin with a blow of its paw. My father said that this was a good thing, because the man Shin would not want to be alive with the thoughts of his family and what the bear had done.

'The bear then stood on its back legs in front of my father, expecting him to quake before it, for the bear likes above all else to instil fear in its enemies. But my father did not quake.

'Instead he said to the bear, "Bear, you have done evil here, beyond what is in even your nature to do. Go now with the man Shin's bullet inside you, so you may remember the evil that you did, and leave this land and live in some other place and eat only nuts and fruit and carrion. Do this and I shall spare your life, and beyond that you shall live for longer than any other bear, and you will only die when my son Makha dies. Otherwise I shall kill you and your soul will be cursed and shall know torment to the end of time."

'And the bear understood this, and left that place, and did not kill again.

'My father brought back the body of the man Shin and the bones of the others so that they could be buried.

'These things are true, for I saw them all with my own eyes, or heard about them from others who were there when they happened.'

When Dersu had translated these last words, the

camp fell silent, and even the river seemed hushed. Frazer wanted to say something, but he didn't know what, and deep inside he knew that there are times when nothing is exactly the right thing to say.

44

Bear and Tiger

The great bear had eaten most of the deer by the time Amba found him. Amba had killed and eaten many bears before – usually black bears that made the mistake of being on the ground and not safely up in a tree, but also the occasional brown bear, caught snoozing in its lair or ambushed on a forest trail.

This bear was huge and there was something ancient and fearsome about it beyond anything Amba had encountered before. But Amba was no coward, and he still wanted to inflict damage on all enemies of the tiger kind.

His method with bears was a modified version of the way he killed big deer – with the added caution of dealing with another predator armed with teeth and claws, rather than just a grass-eater. He would attack from beneath, seizing the throat, and slowly choking the life out of his fearsome prey.

And so, with infinite stealth, Amba stalked the great bear.

The bear was not happy. For so many years now he had been hungry. Somehow the berries and nuts and half-rotten meat he had eaten had not satisfied the emptiness in his stomach, which was perhaps also the emptiness of his soul.

He had a vague memory of other, happier times. Times when he had feasted well, and felt the joy of meat still fresh and blood still warm. But now each day seemed grey and purposeless. And he was often cold. How could that be when it was still summer in the forest? How would he feel when the snows came? Of course he would sleep the long sleep, but then what if he awoke early, with the ground still frozen?

That is what had happened all those years before. He had awoken early and had felt the great hunger, and . . . but no, his old brain was foggy. Had it not been foggy he surely would have heard Amba approach, or smelled the tigerish smell of him.

Amba's ears were flat against his head, his tail low, flicking snake-like from side to side.

Ten metres.

Six metres.

Amba paused – every muscle taut and tense and hard as steel.

He leapt. But as his back paws bit into the ground a twig snapped.

The great bear turned towards the sound, and so when Amba tried to close his jaws round the throat his teeth sank into the bear's massive shoulder muscles. The bear reared and cuffed and bit at Amba, hurling its huge bulk around the clearing.

Amba was now in as much danger as the bear. If the bear got a grip with its own crushing jaws, then the tiger would surely perish.

But Amba had other weapons besides his teeth. He now raked the bear's belly with his vicious back claws, sharp as sushi knives. The claws tore through the skin, tearing great gashes in the bear's most vulnerable spot.

The bear was hurt, so badly hurt, and Amba felt that the battle was his. It was time for the killing bite. He released the grip he had on the bear's shoulder and got ready to sink his teeth into the throat.

It was a mistake.

Had he just kept his grip and continued to rip away with his claws, the bear would soon have tired and died from loss of blood and shock.

But now, as Amba released his grip, the bear had just enough strength for one last swipe with its paw. All its ancient bulk and strength went into the blow, and the force of it hurled Amba back across the clearing. And, summoning all of its remaining strength, the bear roared and charged after the tiger.

Amba, winded and bruised, decided that this was a fight he did not want, and fled before the brown bellowing monster.

The bear did not follow for long. It had taken a mortal wound. It dragged its weary, bleeding body back to its lair – a cave scraped from the dry earth between the roots of an oak tree even older than the bear. It lay down and licked at the cuts and deep gashes.

As it licked its chest, a bullet dropped out – the tiger had bitten right where the bullet had been lodged. It was a bullet from an old Russian army rifle of a kind not used for many, many years.

And when the bullet dropped from the old bear's body, so an ancient pain passed from him, and for the last time the Ussuri giant closed his dark eyes, and slept, forever now untroubled by the old dreams.

But what of Amba? Tiger flesh is tough, and so, once again, as with the bullet, his pride was hurt more than his body.

Humiliation whipped his fury, and now he made his way through the forest with death in his heart. And then he stopped.

There was a scent.

Faint, but definitely there. The smell of humans. One he recognized straight away: the smell of a human girl child.

He turned and followed the scent.

45

The Night in the Forest

Back at the campsite all was quiet. Amazon and Frazer were in their sleeping bags in the small tent. The ground was uneven, and Amazon was tossing and turning, trying to get comfortable. Frazer, more used to the whole camping experience, was already in the pleasant dozy stage just before sleep, when good thoughts – if you are lucky – drift in and out of your mind like white clouds in a summer sky.

Then Amazon heard a very strange noise – a sort of droning song accompanied by a rattling sound. She elbowed Frazer awake, and together they poked their heads out of the tent.

The old tracker was sitting by the fire. He had a stick in one hand that had shells attached to it, threaded on a string. It was the stick that was making the rattling sound. With his other hand he was holding what looked like a tambourine to his mouth. He was singing into the drum of the tambourine, and that was what was making the strange, unsettling, droning noise.

As he sang, he scattered more of the ledum leaves on the fire, filling the air with their heady fragrance.

Amazon noticed that between Makha and the fire there was that same gruesome little blue-eyed wooden figure, Kasalyanku.

Then Makha took out his hunting knife – a long-bladed weapon with a plain wooden handle, without ornament or any unnecessary embellishment – and carefully used it to pick out some glowing embers from the fire. Soon there were four small dots of orange light balanced on the blade. Then the old tracker stood up, still carrying the embers on his knife. He went in turn to four points equally spaced around their little campsite and placed an ember on the ground, each time calling out a word in his own language.

Amazon looked questioningly over at Dersu, who was squatting at the opening of his shelter.

'It is for protection. My grandfather fears that the bear or Amba will come in the night. But now that he has performed this rite we will be safe.'

Strangely, this news didn't reassure Amazon very much.

'Frazer?' she said.

'Yep?'

'You got your X-Ark ready?'

'Yep.'

'Good.'

46

Amba Returns

Amba knew that he was close. The human scent was strong. But there was that other smell again. The one he did not like. The one that made his mind – usually so sharp, so focused – unclear.

He crept closer to the camp. Tigers use scent to mark their territory and can follow a scent trail, but their primary hunting sense is vision. And now, even though it was pitch-black, Amba was close enough to see the tent with Frazer and Amazon in it, and the lean-to shelter.

It was time, he knew, to leap. He extended his claws, stretching them out to their full length. It was normally something that gave the old assassin great pleasure. But not now.

That smell.

The old man who could see into his soul.

It was no good.

Yet again he was thwarted, and once more he was forced to slink away into the forest, his appetite both for meat and for revenge unsatisfied.

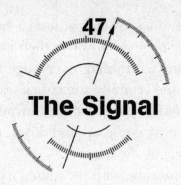

47

The Signal

'Hey, guys, you're not going to believe this, but . . .'

The next morning, after a breakfast of energy bars washed down with sweet tea made from boiled river water, Frazer had decided to try the radio tracking receiver one more time.

Almost immediately there was a blip, and three of the LEDs had lit up on the control panel.

Dersu explained the situation to Makha, who shrugged, and did not look happy. However he did not object to following the electronic trail.

The going was now incredibly tough. Up to this point, apart from the hectic chase after the martens, they had been following forest paths. Some of these had been made by the animals themselves: wild boar, deer, tigers. Some were made long before by the people who had lived here: Russians, Koreans, Chinese, Udege. And even before the Udege had come, a thousand years ago and more, there had been the first inhabitants of this land, the Nivkh.

But now the winding trails were behind them, and

they were heading in straight lines – or as near as they could manage it – towards their target.

That meant scrambling over huge fallen trees, some rotten and crumbly, some slick with moss and lichen. It meant leaping over fast-flowing streams. It meant constantly going up and down, through the different layers of the forest.

It was exhausting, with the added irritant of the constant attacks of horseflies, big as a thumbnail, and evil-looking deer flies, striped black and white, with delta wings like jet fighters. Both would leave an ugly welt when they bit, much more painful than the itchy lumps left by the midges, mosquitoes and blackflies.

When they were walking along the forest trails, Makha had been tireless. But now the old man began to show his age. It was hard for him to scramble over the logs and leap the many brooks, and his grandson often had to stop to help him, while Amazon and Frazer waited.

There was another factor that occurred to Amazon. Perhaps now that he was no longer leading them, Makha felt that he had lost his purpose.

Frazer, however, was far too absorbed in following the signal to pay much attention to anyone else. He kept the aerial high above his head, and watched the control panel so intently that more than once he stumbled and fell. At times the signal strength dropped to one or two out of the five red lights, and once it disappeared altogether. But each time he found a strong signal again.

'We're getting close,' he said to the others, who were strung out behind him. 'I think the leopard is in that clump of oak trees.'

Boris the Dog thought so too. He took it as a sign that it was time to run away. Amazon made a grab for his collar, but the dog was too fast.

'Good riddance,' said Frazer.

48

Tiger Attack!

Some time earlier, Amba had finally found what he was looking for.

There, in front of him, were the female leopard and her two cubs.

So, she thought she was clever, evading him for all this time. The den was a good one: the hollowed-out trunk of a once-mighty fallen larch. Well, now he had her, and those mewling cubs of hers, playing together in the sunshine.

But Amba had to be very careful. A leopard was a formidable opponent. Not as dangerous, perhaps, as a full-grown brown bear, but capable, nevertheless, of inflicting serious damage with claw and tooth. Especially, of course, when she was defending her young. So there was no wild leap from the sly old tiger. He crept through the undergrowth so slowly that he looked to be perfectly immobile, even as he moved.

And the leopard mother was sleepy. She had been

up all night hunting. Normally her senses were so acute that not even a tiger would have been able to creep up on her.

Amba was close now.

He decided that this time he would go for the quick killing bite to the back of the neck – he didn't want to be anywhere near those claws; if he went for the throat grip the leopard might do to *him* what *he* had done to the bear.

It was time. He could smell her now – smell the hateful odour of a rival killer. A rival killer who was now going to play the much more satisfying role of . . . meal.

He leapt.

It was a good leap.

It was better than good – it was perfect.

He was going to land with his front claws sinking into the shoulders, and a micro-second later his canine teeth – ten centimetres of sharp white murder – would cut through the hair and skin, and then sever the leopard's spine, bringing instant death.

And then what fun it would be to toy with those cubs a little before he ate them too.

But just in that moment before he landed he noticed something ever so slightly odd about this leopard.

Odd, and somehow *wrong* . . .

49

A Nasty Surprise

Makha and Dersu were almost as silent as the tiger as they crept through the forest. Frazer and Amazon couldn't match their stealth, but they did their best.

Frazer had turned the sound off on the radio receiver and was relying on the red lights to direct them: all five lights were blazing now.

Amazon felt her pulse race, and tried to control it, as she knew that staying calm was the secret of accurate shooting. She had the X-Ark, loaded up with a fresh carbon dioxide canister and a tranq dart. There might only be one chance, and she had to take it.

Makha put up his hand, and they all stopped dead. Then the old man turned and beckoned Amazon and Frazer forward. With infinite care he opened up a gap in the leaves and pointed a stubby finger.

Amazon couldn't see anything for a moment, and so she brought the X-Ark's telescopic sight up to her eye. Everything was blurry. She twisted the focus ring.

And then suddenly her eye found another eye: closed.

It didn't look right. It didn't seem at all *leopardy*. And then the eye opened, yellow and intense and angry. It looked straight back at Amazon, and Amazon realized that this was no leopard.

It was a tiger.

An angry tiger, just woken from a fitful sleep.

An angry tiger with scratches all over its face, as if it had recently been in a serious fight.

With a savage snarl the tiger sprang towards her.

'Shoot now!' yelled Frazer, who, not looking through the scope, had a wider view of what was going on.

The tiger was twenty metres away, and covering the ground with astonishing speed.

Amazon had no time to think.

She found the tiger's shoulder in the scope and pulled the trigger.

She was sure that her aim was good, but still the tiger came on.

Had she missed? If she had, the consequences would be fatal. It was leaping; it would land among them, perhaps even right on top of Amazon. And then she felt a hard shove. It was Frazer. He'd pushed her aside, and the movement had placed him right under the claws.

Frazer's thinking had been clear. On this, her first mission, Amazon was under his protection, and if

anyone was going to get mauled it wasn't going to
be her. Well, that's how he would have explained it.
In fact, he acted without any real thought at all, other
than the selfless urge to protect.

From the ground, Amazon saw a flash as Makha,
suddenly a man again in his prime, pulled out his
long hunting knife. He was going to fight the fiend
hand-to-claw.

She wanted to cry out, 'No!' She did not want

either Frazer or the old man or even the tiger to be hurt. But nor did she want to die.

And nor did Frazer. His eye had also caught the glint of Makha's knife, so all he saw was a blur of black and gold as the tiger landed right in front of him. Instinctively, he hurled himself backwards, away from the claws and teeth, but as he fell he cracked his head on a rock.

In books and films you often see people knocked unconscious with a blow to the head. In fact it's very hard to knock someone out, and if you do there's a very good chance you'll kill them.

So Frazer wasn't knocked out by the crack to his skull, but he was dazed, and his head filled with light like an extraordinarily intense, if short-lived, firework display.

But he was a fighter, and, through the fug that had invaded his brain after the fireworks went out, he kicked and punched frantically. And then he realized that he was kicking and punching at thin air.

He opened his eyes.

Amazon and Dersu were looking at him, while Makha stood over the body of the tiger lying at Frazer's feet.

For a second he thought that the old man had killed the beast, which filled him with as much misery as relief. He was supposed to be an animal saviour, not killer.

And then he saw the dart in the tiger's shoulder.

'Good shot, Zonnie,' he said, smiling through the pain.

'Believe me,' Amazon replied, 'if I could have arranged it so that I saved your life by shooting you in the butt, then I would have.'

50

In the Belly of the Beast

Frazer stood up and felt gingerly at the back of his head. There was a lump the size of a quail's egg, but no blood. He felt good for a couple of seconds, and then his brain began to work.

Tiger.

Not leopard.

How?

The four of them now stood round the magnificent animal, snoring contentedly. Or at least it sounded contented . . .

'I don't get it,' he said, although as soon as the words were out he'd begun to.

'Does it mean that the leopard is still somewhere close?' said Amazon.

'I've a horrible feeling it does,' replied Frazer.

He picked up the radio receiver and pointed the aerial at the tiger. As soon as he flicked the 'on' switch, all five red lights burst into life and the unit issued forth a manic bleeping. Even though he already knew what this meant, Frazer couldn't resist the morbid urge to move the aerial over the tiger's belly. The beeps increased to the point where Frazer thought the unit was going to blow.

Frazer and Amazon looked at each other.

'Well,' said Frazer. 'We found her.'

Amazon's eyes were wet with tears. 'All this for nothing.'

There was a silence of a couple of seconds, and then Dersu spoke up.

'The leopard had cubs.'

'But wouldn't the tiger have killed the cubs?' There was hope in Amazon's voice, but the hope was as fragile as a thread of spider's silk.

'Mother fight well,' said Dersu, pointing at the scratches on the face of the tiger, and at some deeper gashes on the side. 'Cubs may have been able to run away. If this is so, then my grandfather will find them.'

'What shall we do with this big guy?' Frazer said, more to himself than anyone else.

'I can smell the fire,' said Amazon. 'If we leave him here he may burn . . .'

It was true. The smell of smoke was stronger than ever.

'I doubt it,' Frazer replied. 'The tranquillizer will only keep him under for half an hour. The flames won't be here by then. If he's got any sense, he'll get out of here. Like Bob Doolins said, tigers are excellent swimmers.'

Dersu spoke with Makha. Then he turned to the others. 'My grandfather does not think that Amba will run away. He thinks that now his spirit desires revenge. The tiger's spirit is great and noble, but if he is offended, if his . . . honour is at stake, then he is an enemy without pity. My grandfather says that this is the same tiger with whom he had a conversation back at his home. He does not think that Amba will forgive.'

'So what are you saying?' said Amazon, horrified by what she thought Dersu was proposing.

Dersu shrugged. 'My people respect Amba. But a human life is worth more than the life of even as great an animal as the tiger. Back when my father was young, we would have killed the tiger, and apologized to his spirit, and to the Great Spirit, and to the spirit of the fire. So, yes, we would have killed him. But this is not now our way. My grandfather says only that we must be careful.'

'I think we've talked enough,' said Frazer, putting the now redundant radio receiver back in his pack. 'Let's find those cubs.'

51
Dersu's Story

Makha scanned the ground. In a few seconds he had found the tiger's footprints in a patch of soft earth. He said something in his own language. Amazon and Frazer understood it without the need for a translation.

'This way.'

Now that the radio tracking device was put aside, the old hunter was again in his element. He led them on, finding here a broken blade of grass, there the hint of a paw print. And sometimes a spot of blood – although whether the blood was from the unfortunate leopard or the wounded tiger, not even Makha could tell.

And then, after about half an hour, the trail went cold. Makha searched methodically, but he could find nothing.

'Sometimes this can happen,' said Dersu. 'In winter always there is a trail, but now . . . it is hard.'

Amazon looked at Frazer. 'We've got to find the cubs. I can't bear it if we don't.'

As his grandfather scanned the ground back and forth, Dersu began to look thoughtful.

'I think that I would like to tell you about my father.'

'You don't have to,' said Amazon. 'I mean if it's too painful . . .'

'It is painful, but it is necessary. My mother and father were very poor. My father earned money by finding wild ginseng, but the forest was empty of ginseng. And he looked around, and saw that our people, the Udege, as well as the other tribes, the Nanai and the Ulch and the Oroch, were dying. He did not want me to grow up like him, as a poor man from a dying people in a hard country.

'He wanted to send me to school in Moscow so that I could be a teacher or a scientist or some such person. But he had to get the money – a lot of money. So he went into the forest with his gun. My grandfather tried to stop him, but he could not. And my father tracked a tiger. And my father killed the tiger. He sold the tiger's bones to the Chinese, and the skin to a Russian general in Vladivostok, and with the money he sent me away to school, although I did not want to go.

'Because of what he did, my father was shunned by our people. Even my grandfather would not talk to him. And so he went to live in Vladivostok to hide his shame in the crowd. And because he was alone he found comfort in vodka. And one winter morning he was found, lying in the street, frozen to death.

'This is why my grandfather and I try now to protect the forest, to atone for what my father did. I came back from school. I had learnt much, but also forgotten much. My grandfather and grandmother looked after me, and my grandfather taught me again the ways of the forest. This is my story, and the story of my father.'

Amazon's eyes were glistening. She wanted to say something, but she could not speak. It was too sad. Surprisingly, it was Frazer who spoke up.

'Dersu, if we all carried around the sins of our fathers on our backs, then we'd all look like your grandmother. You've got your own life to lead, and it looks to me that you're making a good job of it. And I've just had a brilliant idea. Why don't you –'

A Return and a Discovery

Frazer never finished his sentence, for at that moment they heard heavy steps, followed by a snuffling noise. For a moment Amazon thought that it might be the tiger, woken from its sleep and back on the warpath. But that fear didn't last long.

'Boris the Dog,' she groaned as the big dog came into view. But she still couldn't stop herself from smiling a little, and she squeezed his fat face and stroked his floppy ears, despite the drool that fell on her.

The big cowardly dog had returned, no doubt feeling that it was safer to be in company in the woods.

'I know he's about as useless as a dog can get,' said Frazer thoughtfully, 'but couldn't he employ that big wet nose of his to sniff out the trail?'

'Worth a try,' said Amazon without much enthusiasm. Boris wasn't the sort of dog to inspire hope.

She took hold of him firmly by the collar.

'Come on, then, Boris, show us what you can do.'

Boris looked at her uncomprehendingly, with his head on one side.

'Leopard,' she tried.

Nothing.

So she made a growling noise, trying to imitate a leopard's roar.

Still it didn't sink in.

'You might as well try to teach the dumb mutt algebra,' grumbled Frazer.

Makha was watching, half amused. Then Dersu spoke to his grandfather, explaining what was going on. The old tracker smiled and put his hands to his mouth. He then did a perfect leopard roar.

The effect on Boris was immediate: he tried to run away. Luckily Amazon still had a good grip on his collar.

Despite his algebra crack, Frazer decided to have a go.

'Not big,' he said to the dog, speaking very slowly and stretching out his arms wide. 'Small. Baby.' He brought his hands closer together to indicate what he meant.

Amazon tutted loudly. It was her turn to be sarcastic. 'Why not try spelling it out,' she said. 'S-M-A-L-L.'

Of course it may just have been chance, or perhaps one of the circuits in the dog's brain fired randomly, but just then Boris did look more alert. He started to sniff at the forest floor. He made one of his yawning whines, dribbled and drooled even more than usual, and started to drag Amazon along.

'Maybe Boris isn't so stupid after all,' said Frazer.

The four of them followed the dog for a couple of hundred metres. And then Makha stopped. He put his hand to his ear. They all listened. And, yes, there was a mewling sound, somewhere close.

Boris heard it too, and reverted back to coward mode. Even a baby leopard was too much leopard for him, and once again he ran away.

If they'd been paying closer attention, Amazon and Frazer might have noticed something slightly different about this latest act of cowardice, but they were already following the sound. It led them to a fallen tree, rotten and hollow. The sound came from within.

Frazer knew that in normal circumstances what they were doing now would be deadly dangerous. A mother leopard would kill and kill again to protect her young. But the mother leopard was dead, and their mission was now to save the cubs. He reached blindly into the hollow trunk and felt the soft fur of a cub. He also felt a sharp scratch, and pulled his hand out.

'Feisty!' he said, smiling ruefully. He sucked at the scratch, which wasn't bad, and reached again, more carefully this time, into the log. He found the scruff, and pulled out one of the cubs.

Amazon could not stop herself from sighing at the sight of the beautiful little creature. It was a boy, and he seemed to think that it was his job to protect his sister, even though she was bigger and stronger than him. He growled and batted at them with his paws, and tried to nip at Frazer's fingers with his needle-sharp teeth.

'Give him here,' said Amazon, and Frazer was pleased to let the little fighter go.

As soon as he was in Amazon's arms, the cub relaxed. The truth was that he was cold and lonely and missed his mother, and somehow he knew that the creature holding him now would not harm him.

Frazer reached in for the other cub. She took to Frazer just as her brother had taken to Amazon.

Amazon's cub started to suck at her finger. Its tongue was rough, and tickled, but the sensation was delicious.

'Look, they're starving,' she said. 'Is there anything we can give them?'

Frazer was about to reply that he had some powdered milk in his pack, which they could mix up, and that perhaps it would do until they found something better. However, before he had the chance to speak, another voice, booming and huge, came from behind them.

'Anything you can give? Why, yes, give them to me, ha ha.'

53

Boris is Back

Amazon spun round and saw the grinning face of Boris, and the drooling, treacherous face of Boris the Dog, who had clearly led his true master back to them.

Boris the man looked dirty and dishevelled, and the part of his face not already covered by his huge moustache was thickly crusted with black stubble. She also noticed that he had a deep cut over one eye, still oozing a little blood.

But it wasn't the face that caught her attention. It was the gun – Boris's rifle – that was pointing at her chest. Two more men loomed up at Boris's side. Amazon hadn't seen these guys before. They were dressed in the scruffy clothes of hunters who had apparently been in the woods for some time, but something about their silent menace and quiet efficiency made Amazon think that these were professionals, and not weekend hunters out to bag a deer for the pot. One had an AK-47 assault rifle, and the other carried a pump-action shotgun.

Boris the Dog fawned and frolicked around Boris the man.

'Never trusted that mutt,' said Frazer.

'What's going on?' said Amazon. 'Where are the others? Miranda . . .? Bluey . . .?'

'Don't ask Boris question. Just do what Boris say. That way you stay alive, maybe. You tell me now where is old savage and stupid boy.'

Frazer, puzzled, looked around. There was no sign of the two Udege.

It was Amazon who answered. 'They went to carry the female leopard to the rendezvous with Doolins. We tranquillized it earlier. They left us to capture the cubs and bring them down to the boat as soon as we could.'

Frazer looked at her in surprise, and was about to ask her what on earth she was talking about. He stopped himself in the nick of time.

Boris grunted. He spoke in Russian to the other two. They nodded and made off into the forest, evidently in pursuit of the Udeges.

'Now, give small leopards,' said Boris. 'Then we go see your friends. All be fine.' Boris added his usual laugh at the end of this, but there was something false about it. And that false laugh, and what it might imply, was the single most frightening thing about the experience for Amazon.

Amazon thought about running. Frazer thought

about making a grab for Boris's gun. But they both realized it would be suicide. Reluctantly, they walked towards Boris and put the leopard cubs, squirming and squealing, into the sack he held out.

'Boris is sorry for this,' he said, performing one of his elaborate shrugs. 'But Boris also has orders to obey.'

54

Fair is Foul, and Foul is Fair

Boris jabbed them in the back with his Kalashnikov and they began to trudge through the forest. Amazon felt desolate. She didn't fully understand what was happening, but she knew that it was bad. Bad for her. Bad for the others. Bad for the leopard cubs. She faintly hoped that Dersu and Makha might have some plan to rescue them, and that was why they had disappeared. But she couldn't blame them if they had just decided to save themselves. To them they were all outsiders – Russians, American and British alike. People who came to steal their land and destroy their culture.

Different thoughts were passing through Frazer's mind. He had been in plenty of scrapes before. He knew how ruthless poachers could be, and that's what he assumed Boris was – just someone out to kill the leopards to sell their bones and skins to the highest bidder. He knew that Boris would have few worries about killing them as well. And so he was waiting for a chance to turn and surprise the Russian, especially now he was alone. He assumed that Kirov wasn't part of this – he didn't have the look of a poacher. Perhaps Boris had already killed him.

Frazer knew he had to act soon, before they reached the others. He bent to tie his bootlace, meaning to let Boris get closer and then make a grab for the gun.

However, the second he stooped to tie the lace, he felt Boris's big boot crash into his shoulder, leaving him sprawling on the ground.

At the same moment Boris grabbed Amazon. He pulled her down with him next to Frazer. His hot garlicky breath was in her face, and for a second she thought that he was about to kill them both then and there. She began to struggle, but then Boris spoke in an urgent whisper.

'I have only a few seconds for this. Your lives are in deadly danger, as are those of your friends.'

'What's –' began Frazer, but Boris silenced him.

'Listen or you die. I am an agent for the Russian secret service. The man you call Kirov works for a Russian billionaire. This man owns many things, including a logging company. By using bribes and corruption and the killing of those in his way, he was about to obtain permission to cut down the trees in this region. The release of the leopards stopped this because the animals are protected by national laws, and the eyes of the world would be upon them. So it was important not only to kill the leopards here, but also to show that it was pointless to even try to reintroduce them, because of the lawlessness of the region. And so the plan was to kill the naturalists who were helping the leopards, and blame it on bandits and poachers. As soon as the attempt to bring leopards to this area is abandoned, the logging can begin.'

Frazer nodded. 'So what can we do?'

'The choice is yours. I go to try to rescue your friends. Either you run now and attempt to raise the alarm, or you help me. Trouble is there are two more killers with Kirov, as well as the ones who went after the Udege. If I fail, they will hunt you down. But I cannot force you to help me. Is up to you.'

Amazon and Frazer exchanged looks. 'We'll help,' said Amazon decisively. 'But what can we do?'

'You have tranquillizer gun. You can use it to take down one of the guards. It will mean I will have a better chance with the others.'

'You're sure about this?' Frazer said to Amazon.

She nodded. 'Let's do it.'

55

Kirov's Camp

Ten minutes later Boris shoved the two children into a forest clearing. Their hands were tied – or appeared to be tied – behind their backs.

Boris the Dog trotted alongside, sniffing and drooling at every tree without a care.

What the children saw there in the clearing shocked them both to the core. Bluey and Miranda Coverdale were lying awkwardly, their hands and feet bound together. They were both gagged.

Bluey was almost unrecognizable, so battered and bloodied was his face. His eyes were closed. Miranda was very far from the well-groomed and serious person Amazon had first met only a few days before. Her hair hung in ragged tangles across her face, and her clothing was torn and filthy.

Two armed guards, one sitting, one standing, were close to them. Kirov stood quietly by, his face bearing a placid smile.

Boris spoke to him in Russian, and he gave Frazer another shove.

To Amazon's surprise, Kirov answered not in Russian, but in English.

'Ah, Boris, how good to see you.'

Boris's face also registered surprise. And then something in Kirov's tone obviously alerted him to the fact that the game was up. He tried to raise his rifle, but it was too late. Kirov had already drawn his Russian Special Forces issue semi-automatic pistol from a holster under his armpit, and with it he shot the giant calmly in the chest.

Boris dropped his rifle, staggered and pawed at the neat hole in his jacket.

Frazer yelled, 'Noooooo!'

At the same moment, Amazon pulled out the X-Ark, which she'd been clutching behind her back.

She bent to one knee – the perfect stable platform to get in her shot – and aimed for Kirov's neck. One of the guards lunged towards her, but Frazer hurled himself in the way. The guard cuffed him aside, but it gave Amazon the second she needed to get her shot in, and the dart, with its double dose of tranquillizer sped unerringly towards its target.

But another projectile was heading for Kirov's throat. It had finally sunk into the dull brain of Boris the Dog that something bad was happening to his master. He did not understand the nature of guns, and so found no reason not to hurl himself at Kirov, teeth bared, drool flying. Kirov put up his arm in a reflexive gesture, but there was no need: Amazon's well-aimed dart sank into the back of the dog's thick skull, and he hit the ground already unconscious.

There was no time for another shot. One of the guards gave Amazon a vicious backhanded slap across the face, and twisted the gun from her hands.

Boris, who still had not fallen, made a desperate lunge at Kirov, but he was moving like a drunk man. Kirov permitted him to take a couple of unsteady steps in his direction, and then calmly sent another bullet into his chest.

This time the shot knocked Boris from his feet into an ungainly, almost comical sitting position. The look on his grizzled face was more one of amazement than pain. Then he slumped backwards, and lay on the leaf-strewn ground, staring up into the branches of the trees that ringed the clearing. A ghastly gurgling sound emerged from his mouth.

Kirov chuckled and stood over him. He gave him a kick, and, satisfied that there was no fight left in the big man, put the pistol back in its holster. Then he reached into his jacket and took out a folding pocket-knife. He bent and used the knife to cut the fabric of Boris's jacket collar. A small object, about the size of a shirt button, appeared in his palm.

'Microphone, old friend,' he said, and gave Boris an affectionate Russian slap on the cheek. 'You are not the only one trained in the methods of the good old KGB. I heard every word. But it only served to confirm my suspicions.'

Boris tried to speak, but could manage nothing more than incomprehensible, barely human sounds.

Amazon moved to help him, but a guard's powerful hand grabbed her. She twisted and fought to free herself from the grip, and bit at the hand that held her, but the guard was strong and he knew what he was doing. Amazon gave up the struggle.

Kirov barked an order, and the guards tied the children's hands behind their backs – properly, this time – and forced them to kneel.

A final straining sound came from Boris, as if he had something of vital importance to say.

And then silence.

The sack with the squirming cubs lay by his side.

Amazon found that she was crying.

Kirov watched Boris die with a sort of curious indifference, and then he turned to the children.

Blip!

'So, you know the truth. I do not begrudge that a person should have knowledge of the reason for which they die. When I was in the KGB we always convinced those whom we were to execute that it was for the good of the Soviet Union, and of mankind, and therefore of themselves. Such knowledge can be a comfort.'

'You don't have to do this,' said Amazon through her tears. 'You've got the leopards. You could just let us go . . .'

'Don't waste your breath,' said Frazer bitterly. He could see that there was no way this man would let them live.

Kirov smiled, not unsympathetically.

'My dear child, I honestly wish that I could let you go. I get no joy from killing you. However, my employer does not like loose ends. And two children with the knowledge that you have, not to mention your friends here –' he gestured with his thumb towards Miranda and Bluey – 'would certainly be considered loose ends.'

Frazer had begun to despair. But now he heard something that at first puzzled him, and then gave him a shred of hope. He was still wearing his backpack, and from deep within it he heard the faintest of blips. A couple of seconds later it was followed by another – still faint, but definitely louder. It wasn't much, but it was enough to make him want to keep Kirov talking for a little longer.

'Is all this really just about logging rights?' he asked.

'*Just* logging rights? Have you any idea how much all of these fine ancient larch and pine trees are worth? Millions of dollars. But, no, you are quite correct. It is not *simply* the timber. My employer is a man who sees all things as connected. And nothing is wasted. These cubs here, for example, will, in time, serve my employer's – how do you say it? – *hobby*.'

Another blip. Louder, definitely louder.

'Hobby? What are you talking about?'

'You are not the only ones with a love of wild things. My employer has a large reserve for rare and endangered animals.'

Frazer was baffled. This didn't seem to make sense. But at least Kirov was still talking.

'You mean he breeds them . . . to release back into the wild?'

'Breed? Release? Oh no, you quite misunderstand. He hunts them. The rarer the creature, the more intense the thrill of the chase.'

Another blip. Loud enough for Frazer to worry that Kirov might hear it too.

'What do you have?' he asked hurriedly.

'White rhinos, Arabian oryx, Bengal tigers . . . Mr Kaggs, er, I mean my employer, has shot them all. And these little fellows here will grow up to be fine trophies.'

'*You* are the animals,' spat Amazon.

Frazer would have kicked her if he'd been close enough. The last thing he wanted now was to anger Kirov. They had to keep him talking.

Blip.

'Of course,' replied Kirov with placid amusement. 'We are animals. You, me, my employer. Members of the species *Homo sapiens*. Descended from the apes. And immortality is a gift denied to all the members of the animal kingdom.' He sniffed at the air. The smell of smoke was now ever present. 'And it seems that our time is limited. Once again, my apologies.'

He cocked the pistol, raised it and Amazon stared down the barrel, unable to believe the inevitable truth that her life was about to end.

Old Friends

Kirov paused, his finger on the trigger.

'What is that noise?' he enquired. The beeps had become an almost constant sound now.

In a flash Amazon realized the significance of the beeps: the radio tracking device! Something was coming. Something that might kill them horribly.

Or possibly save them.

Frazer was about to say something – anything – to drag the conversation out, but he stopped, dumbfounded.

On the edge of the clearing he saw a figure. But it was difficult to see clearly. The day was growing darker now, both with the gathering dusk and the smoke coming from the fire. The figure looked like Makha, the old Udege. But it was a Makha strangely transformed. He seemed taller and younger, yet also less solid, like a figure in a dream.

He stood with his arms outstretched, the smoke swirling around him, the forked staff held in his right hand. And he was singing that strange, nasal song. As before, the sound made the hairs on the back of Frazer's neck stand up.

The Russians heard it too, and all turned to face the new arrival. Kirov's mouth fell open. But he was not a man to remain stunned for long. He trained the pistol on the smoke-wreathed figure, and fired off three shots.

Bang.

Bang.

Bang.

Somehow he managed to miss, or so it appeared, as the Udege continued his song uninterrupted. Kirov checked his weapon, cocked it and fired again, more hurriedly this time.

Bangbangbangbang.

Frazer couldn't be sure, but he thought that the old man, who now appeared ageless, smiled.

And then he was no longer standing there at the border between the clearing and the thick, mysterious forest.

Where had he gone? How had he vanished?

There was no time, however, to wonder over this. The space once filled by Makha was now ablaze with living fire: not the burning forest, but the great tiger, Amba, who leapt into the clearing with a snarl like the ripping of the very fabric of the universe.

The Russian guards fired wildly, screamed and fled away into the forest, leaving their guns behind them.

Kirov, made of sterner stuff, fired again and again at the tiger with his pistol. The retorts only succeeded in attracting the attention of Amba. The tiger, who had begun to chase the guards into the forest, turned and began to move towards Kirov, still snarling out his rage.

Kirov pulled the trigger again, with the tiger only a few metres away, but this time there was nothing but a sharp click, indicating that the pistol's twelve-round magazine was empty.

Finally, realizing his peril, Kirov hurled his now useless weapon at the tiger and turned to follow his comrades. The tiger leapt after him, and both disappeared into the depth of the forest.

Seconds later, Frazer and Amazon heard a terrified scream, choked off into silence.

58

Out of the Frying Pan . . .

'Are you OK?' Frazer called to Amazon.

She was shaking, cold and in shock, but she managed to nod her head. Yet she knew that they were still in deadly danger. The tiger was on the loose, and the fire was getting ever closer, and their hands were all still bound.

And then, emerging at the spot previously occupied by Makha, another, slighter figure appeared.

'Dersu!' cried Amazon. 'I knew you'd come. You brought the tiger here, didn't you?'

'Yes, that was my grandfather's plan,' he replied, moving quickly to cut through the ropes tying their wrists. 'We led the two Russians deep into the forest, where they became lost. I do not think that we will meet with them again . . . And then we drew Amba here. First I ran before Amba, and then I climbed a tree while my grandfather led him the rest of the way.'

'But your grandfather . . . he was here . . . and then . . . he wasn't.'

'Please tell me exactly what you saw,' Dersu said quietly, but with an intense emotion, impossible to miss.

'Sure,' said Frazer, picking up the discarded X-Ark. 'But first let me reload this baby. I don't fancy being the dessert course for that tiger.'

And then Amazon and Frazer together tried to explain what they had seen, although suddenly it seemed insane to them both.

Dersu shook his head, as if he were denying something. Amazon thought she saw a tear glisten in the corner of his eye, although that may have been because of the smoke.

'I think that my grandfather has gone,' he said, his voice flat and toneless. 'There was the fire . . . He could not have escaped.'

'But what we saw . . .?'

'I do not know. Perhaps it was a trick of the smoke, of the fire. Or perhaps it was my father,' he said simply. 'I mean, that he came to help my grandfather. And now they have returned together to the Great Spirit.'

'I don't understand,' said Amazon.

'It was his time. He had lived for long enough. He wanted to be again with my father in the spirit world, and my father came to meet him.'

Frazer put his hand on the older boy's shoulder. 'Are you OK?' he asked.

Dersu nodded, wiped his eyes with his sleeve, and said: 'Now we must help your friends . . .'

It was only then that Amazon remembered Miranda and Bluey. Dersu cut their hands and wrists free, while Amazon undid the gags. Bluey was groggy from the beating he'd taken, and Miranda's eyes were still wild. But she soon recovered her coolness.

'Thanks,' she said. 'Boris told me about the plot as soon as we were on our own. He said he did not know who he could trust. He even suspected Doolins. But then Kirov showed up with those other Russians. They'd been lying in wait for us in the forest. They'd already beaten up poor Bluey. They only kept us alive so that we could use the radio tracking equipment to find the leopards.'

'Oh, Boris,' wailed Amazon. It was all too much for her, and now she could feel the tears rolling down her cheeks.

They all went to the side of the fallen giant.

'Is he . . .?' Frazer began.

Miranda gave a quick shake of her head. 'It's too late for him. We've got to get out of here. We can still make it to the rendezvous. Bob Doolins should be there. We've got to keep the leopards safe. They're what really matters now. The cubs . . .?'

Amazon felt in the old sack and took out one of the cubs. It was the male, and it seemed to recognize her, and growled affectionately. Frazer took out 'his' cub.

'They're still hungry,' he said.

He was interrupted by a voice that, although weak, nevertheless somehow managed to resound like a wave crashing on a rocky shore.

'Boris also hungry. Getting shot is good for appetite, ha ha.'

The children leapt back in surprise, and then pressed forward again, delightedly.

'You're . . . you're . . .' stammered Amazon.

'Impossible,' said Miranda. 'I saw Kirov shoot you.'

Bluey popped a button on Boris's shirt, revealing a black layer of fabric.

'Bullet-proof vest!'

Boris heaved himself up on his elbows. He was clearly in considerable pain.

'Of course. Boris is professional. But swine Kirov used armour-piercing shells. Vest did not stop all bullet. Broken ribs and small hole of bullet. But takes more than one bullet hole to kill Boris!'

He broke off into a torrent of coughing. Finally he spat. He looked at the spit. It was red.

'Maybe Boris not so good.'

Miranda attended to him, using a field dressing from Frazer's pack.

'Hate to rush you guys,' said Bluey, 'but we've got to get out of here. That fire's going to catch up with us any moment now.'

And for the first time Frazer could see the red glow of the approaching flames.

And then something even more fearsome caught his sharp eye: the snarl of white teeth.

For a second he thought it was the returning tiger, and dread filled his soul. But then he realized that it was something smaller than the tiger, if no less fierce.

59
Frazer's Chance

It was the mother leopard.

And Frazer was holding one of her precious babies.

Frazer was filled with two totally opposite emotions: joy at the fact that, against all the odds and all the evidence, the leopard was still alive; and terror about what she would do.

Frazer could see that the leopard's muscles were tensed and ready to spring – but perhaps she was also in two minds. Would the humans hurt her babies before she reached them?

No one else had seen the leopard yet, and Frazer realized he had only seconds in which to act.

He thrust the cub he was holding into Amazon's arms, where it joined its sibling. He knew that he was putting her in danger, but he had to do it if he were to save them all.

Then he hurled himself towards the cast-aside X-Ark. Out of the corner of his eye he saw that the leopard had made the decision that a leopard will always make: to attack!

He swept up the X-Ark and went into a roll. There was no time to aim properly – in fact he was still rolling when he fired.

Amazon had seen all this with amazement. She thought briefly that Frazer had gone mad. And now the X-Ark dart was flying straight at her face. Except that it zipped just past her ear, with the sound of an angry hornet.

The leopard, caught in the moment before it made its spring, halted, staggered and fell.

Bluey, Miranda and Amazon all stared in astonished silence at Frazer and at the sleeping cat. And then they all burst out laughing: partly in relief that no one had been hurt and, in Amazon and Frazer's case, amazement at the fact that the leopard was still alive.

'We thought that the tiger had killed her,' Frazer explained to the others. 'The radio collar – look it's been torn off. The tiger must have attacked her and swallowed it. The collar probably saved her life.'

It was Dersu who brought them all back down to ground. 'Maybe saved her life, then, but now unless you hurry, all will die.'

He was right. The fire was now pressing on three sides against the clearing. 'But how can we . . .' Amazon stammered. 'The leopard . . . Boris . . .'

'Boris, you leave,' gasped the Russian giant. 'Cannot carry. Even if you could, would slow down. All burn. Go, but give Boris his gun.'

'I hate to say it, Amazon,' said Miranda, in her usual cool and collected way, 'but he's right. Unless we run for it now, we will all die here.'

60

When the Stars Threw Down Their Spears and Watered Heaven with Their Tears

'No!' Amazon yelled, hurriedly putting the cubs back in the sack. 'There must be a way.'

She looked from face to face. No one met her eye. They all knew the truth of what Miranda had said. The flames were everywhere now, and she could feel the fire's hot breath on her face.

The silence was broken by Boris. 'Go! Go! Go! I will not have death of children on conscience. Already is much.'

And then Frazer spoke up. 'Amazon's right. We've got to try.'

He put his arm round the Russian. Amazon did the same on the other side. Boris still smelled of garlic sausage, but now there was blood also on his breath. Together they heaved. Dersu joined them, while Bluey and Miranda went for the leopard.

'We must hurry,' said Dersu. 'Only reaching the river can save us now.'

And then the Udege paused. His incredibly sharp

senses had picked something up. Amazon heard it too. And then Frazer. They looked up into the sky.

'What is it?' asked Miranda. 'Wait, no, I hear it . . . an aeroplane.'

'Not a plane,' said Bluey. 'Helicopter. More than one, I think.'

And then they saw it: a huge, fat-bellied, Russian Mi-26 helicopter – the largest in the world – circling two hundred metres above them. And now the thundering scream of its eight-bladed rotor was deafening. There was a huge bucket-like thing dangling beneath it, suspended by two thick cables.

And the Mi-26 was not alone. Two more. No, three were circling along with it.

'What's going on?' Amazon screamed into Frazer's ear.

'I don't know,' he yelled back. 'Oh, hang on, I think I've got it. We should –'

He never finished. One of the two cables holding the enormous bucket was shortened, which had the effect of tipping it up and emptying out fifteen thousand litres of water on to the forest below. Had it landed directly on the clearing, it would have pounded the group to death, and if any had survived, it would have drowned them. But the water was aimed at the fire raging outside the clearing.

As it was, muddy waters coursed around them in a brown torrent. Frazer and Amazon had to lift

Boris's torso up out of the flow to save him, while Bluey and Miranda struggled with the awkward weight of the leopard.

Boris the Dog, however, required no help – at the first splash, he shook his head, climbed groggily to his feet, and then doggy-paddled until the water drained away.

The other helicopters delivered their own thunderous loads in the surrounding forest, and soon billows of steamy water vapour had replaced the choking smoke of the fire.

It was hellish and fun at the same time – although the fun part only began when they realized they weren't about to be drowned.

Twice the helicopters chugged away, only to reappear minutes later – Frazer guessed that they had gone to replenish their cargo of water by dipping the gigantic buckets in the nearby river.

'Who do you think it is?' said Amazon, to no one and everyone at the same time.

'Doolins, maybe,' said Bluey. 'He could have got a sniff of the trouble that was brewing here and called in some help.'

'I don't think Bob had the authority to call in the big guns like this,' said Miranda. 'Those are Russian government helicopters.'

'That one's getting closer,' said Frazer, raising his voice again to be heard over the roaring engine. They all felt the powerful downdraught from the huge rotor blades, and ducked, even though the helicopter was still a hundred metres above them.

'It's landing,' said Bluey. 'Get back, everyone.'

He was right. The big yellow chopper eased down in the clearing. There was just enough room, and Frazer couldn't help but admire the skill of the pilot.

Nevertheless they were all on their guard. Too many bad things had happened for them to glibly assume that these were the cavalry come to save them.

A door on the side of the Mi-26 screeched back, and a figure, muscular but well past the first flush of youth, jumped out, ignoring the ladder that had been lowered before him. His hair was shaved close to his skull, military style. His eyes were grey, and troubled.

'Dad!'

61

Rescued

Frazer ran over to Hal Hunt and they hugged a little awkwardly, as if neither of them were overly familiar with such intimacy.

'You got the leopards?' said Hal, looking anxiously around.

'We sure did, Dad. A mother and two cubs. But we've taken some casualties. We need to get Boris – the big guy over there on the ground – to hospital as soon as possible. He's taken a bullet or two.'

'What?'

'Long story. I'll fill you in when we get going. But how did you know . . .? I mean . . . and where did you get these helicopters from?'

The others had come up to join them, and more figures were climbing out of the helicopter.

'As soon as I found out what was going on,' his father said, 'I got in touch with Bob Doolins. He gave me a briefing, and said that the fire was moving more quickly than they expected. We pulled some strings at the Russian Interior Ministry. Strings with a couple of million roubles attached . . .'

He was interrupted by Amazon, her eyes full of yearning. And fear.

'Uncle Hal?'

'Oh, gee, Dad,' said Frazer. 'I forgot, you haven't even met Amazon yet, have you?'

'Amazon,' said Hal Hunt, in a voice somehow equally conveying sadness and joy. 'You've grown . . . When I last saw you, you were still in diapers.'

'My mum and dad . . .? Did you . . .?'

Hal Hunt held her shoulders. His face was deadly serious.

'I'm sorry, Amazon. The news isn't great. Your parents never showed up in Vancouver. There's no record of their flight path, or whether they landed anywhere else. There's no need to panic yet, but . . .'

Amazon tried to keep her voice calm. 'You think there was an accident?'

'It's probably just that they changed their plans. That brother of mine was never very predictable. Either way, we'll find them, Amazon. I swear it.' Hal paused and surveyed the devastation around. He shook his head and continued: 'But look, let's get you all to safety. That's the important thing now. And you can tell me what's been going on here.'

Frazer was the last one to climb into the helicopter,

urging Dersu up the ladder in front of him. The young Udege had been putting on a brave face, but Frazer could see that he was devastated by the loss of his grandfather.

As he pulled the door shut, he looked for the last time around the clearing. And he saw something: a shambling figure, emerging from the burnt and steaming forest. At first Frazer thought it must be Kirov or one of the other Russian killers, and he called out to his father. But then he realized that this stooped and aged man could only be one person.

'Dersu!' he shouted above the din of the helicopter motor. 'It's your grandfather!'

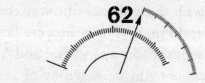

62

A New Tracker . . . and an Old Enemy

In the helicopter, Dersu tried to explain what his grandfather told him.

'He said he led Amba on towards where you were, as we planned. But his legs were too old, and his breathing was bad because of the smoke from the fire. He could not reach the clearing, and he fell down before Amba and expected to die. And Amba gloried over him in his victory. And my grandfather's grief was not for his own life, but for those of the young people. But then a vision came to him. It was of his son, my father, who had been lost. And Amba followed my father's spirit, and he led him to you.'

And when the others looked sceptical he said, 'This is what my grandfather believes, and he has lived for more than seventy years and never told a lie.'

And, looking at the old man, they all knew that he was not lying, whatever the truth might be.

*

The parting with the leopards was very emotional for Amazon and Frazer. The helicopter flew them to a safe place in the forest, and Hal and Miranda carried the mother to the tangled roots of an ancient oak, while Amazon and Frazer carried the cubs.

Bluey attached a new radio collar to the sleeping leopardess.

'One of these saved your neck before,' he said, 'and it might do again.'

Amazon and Frazer gave the cubs a final cuddle, and then nestled them in close to their mother's body. They didn't have long, as the leopardess was showing the first signs of coming round, and she was unlikely to be grateful if she found them still there when she awoke.

'Job well done, guys,' said Hal.

'They will be safe here, won't they?' Amazon asked.

'I reckon so,' Hal replied, putting his hand reassuringly on her arm. 'I'll make sure the reintroduction programme gets more funding from TRACKS and, now that the central government knows what's been going on here, there shouldn't be any more trouble from the loggers and poachers.'

'When my dad says something, he means it,' Frazer added.

And then they all jumped as the leopardess twitched.

'Time to scram,' said Bluey, and they hurried back to the helicopter. Amazon was the last to climb through the door, and she looked back to see the leopardess sleepily licking at her mewling babies.

Next they took Dersu and Makha back to their house. The old man seemed much frailer than he had done just two days before. His wife – whose name they had finally discovered was Ludmilla – came out and scolded him, and then led him back towards the house.

Hal Hunt shook Dersu's hand and said, 'Young man, I've a lot to thank you and your grandfather for. You saved the lives of my son and my niece, as well as the leopards. I'd like to ask you formally to join our organization. TRACKS badly needs people like you.'

'That's exactly what I was going to suggest!' said Frazer.

Dersu looked excited for a moment, but then his face fell.

'I must stay here to care for my grandparents . . .'

'But this is precisely where we want you, for now,' said Hal. 'Bob Doolins needs a right-hand man. There'll be money to help your people, and later, when you're . . . well, when you're freer, you can come out and join us properly. I can guarantee you an interesting life.'

Dersu smiled broadly. 'This is a good plan,' he said.

Amazon and Frazer hugged him, and then he went to stand beside his grandparents. The three of them waved as the helicopter heaved itself heavily into the sky.

Finally, they flew back to the Russian military base in Vladivostok.

Boris was rushed to hospital, yelling out a final, 'Boris will be back, ha ha,' as he was wheeled away.

On the plane from Seoul to Vancouver, Hal Hunt got them to tell the story all over again from the beginning.

'The name,' he said, his lean face hard to read. 'The employer of this man Kirov. Did he mention it?'

'I think he did,' said Frazer. 'Crags, maybe. Something like that.'

'Not Crags,' said Amazon. 'It was Kaggs.'

Hal nodded, as if it were something he was expecting.

In fact, it was a name he hadn't heard for more than forty years, and it filled him with dread. But he did not speak of this to the others. It was not the time. Now was the time to sleep.

And Frazer drifted off in the comfortable first-class seat, reliving that brilliant shot with the X-Ark, the one that saved Amazon from the leopard.

Amazon thought only of her parents.

She knew that they were alive, somewhere out there. And she knew that she was going to help find them.

TOP 10 FACTS: THE AMUR LEOPARD

1. There are nine living subspecies of leopard, of which the **AMUR LEOPARD** is the most endangered.

2. There are only about 30 **AMUR LEOPARDS** left in the wild, and about 200 **AMUR LEOPARDS** in zoos.

3. Although it used to range over a much larger territory, the **AMUR LEOPARD** is now confined to a small area on the borders of North Korea, China and Russia.

4. The **AMUR LEOPARD** has a much thicker coat than other leopards, and a longer tail. The thick coat makes it look larger than it is – it is actually quite small for a leopard.

5. Although the most rapacious man-eater in history was a leopard, which killed more than 400 people in India, there are no records of the **AMUR LEOPARD** ever having killed a human being.

6. The **AMUR LEOPARD** can leap six metres horizontally and three metres vertically.

7. In the wild the **AMUR LEOPARD** mainly eats deer and wild pigs, but it will also hunt smaller prey, such as hares and badgers.

8. A mother **AMUR LEOPARD** will usually have two or three cubs in the spring. The cubs will stay with her for up to two years.

9. The main threats to the **AMUR LEOPARD** are loss of habitat, as its forests are cut down, or burned; the scarcity of prey as a result of human hunting; and illegal poaching for its skin and body parts, which are used in traditional Chinese medicine.

10. Preparations are underway for the reintroduction of the **AMUR LEOPARD** to the Sikhote-Alin region of the Russian Far East, where the action of *LEOPARD ADVENTURE* takes place.

If you want to help save the species, you can adopt an **AMUR LEOPARD** here:

support.wwf.org.uk

Shark Adventure . . . a sneak peek!

Trouble in the Lagoon

Amazon and Frazer were supposed to be keeping an eye on the beach, alert to the first sign that the baby turtles were hatching, but the morning was simply too perfect to just sit and stare at the sand.

Frazer looked at Amazon, a bright light sparkling in his grey eyes.

'Race you,' he said, and sprinted away over the beach towards the glassy waters of the lagoon.

'*Cheat,*' yelled Amazon. She was right on his heels, but Frazer's head start meant that he hit the sea a second or two before her. The beach shelved gently, and Frazer's heels kicked up the spray into her face for ten strides before the water was deep enough for him to hurl himself into a flat dive.

The lagoon retained a little of its night-time coolness, but it was still the warmest seawater Amazon had ever set foot in. It didn't stop her from gasping when Frazer came up and swept a great armful of spray into her face.

'Look!' yelled Frazer, pointing across the lagoon. 'It's a –'

'Dolphin!'

A sleek, grey-green shape rose once, twice, and then disappeared again.

Like a lot of girls her age, Amazon had been obsessed with dolphins as long as she could remember. In her dreams sometimes she would become a dolphin, carving her way through the water, leaping into the air, effortlessly free and happy. It was the perfect way to forget the misery of the long journey here.

'But what's it doing here?' Frazer asked. 'I thought the lagoon was too shallow at low tide for anything that large?'

'It must have become trapped,' said Amazon. 'It should be OK until the tide rises again, and it can get out over the reef, or through the gap we came through last night. In fact, I don't understand why it hasn't already found the gap. Perhaps it's fishing.'

And then the dolphin breached again, this time leaping clear of the water. Now they could see that it was not alone. A miniature copy followed its every move, like a shadow on the sunlit water.

'It's a baby!' sighed Amazon. 'And it looks like a few more dolphins are in the lagoon as well,' she said, spying more dark shapes just below the water, and the odd fin breaking the surface.

Then they were distracted by the sound of voices calling from the shore.

Frazer waved back at the women and children who had come down to the edge of the water.

'What are they saying?' asked Amazon.

'I have no idea,' replied Frazer. 'My Polynesian is a little rusty. But it looks like we'll soon find out.' Two of the older children were pushing a small canoe over the sand.

A loud yackity, clicking noise drew their attention back to the dolphins. Up until now, Amazon had thought that the mother and baby dolphin had been simply playing in the lagoon, but now she noticed that there was something strange in their behaviour. They were darting back and forth in an agitated manner, as if they were frightened.

'I think they're getting a bit panicked by all this action,' she said. 'Maybe we should head back to the beach and check out the turtle eggs.'

Before Frazer had the chance to answer they heard excited shouting. It was the children in the canoe. There was a boy, who looked to be about the same age as them, and a younger child. They were pushing the canoe along, using stout bamboo poles.

'You! Get out of water! Climb on boat!' said the boy.

'What? Why?' said Frazer. 'We mean the dolphins no harm.'

'Not only dolphins in sea. Sharks! Many.'

Amazon felt a cold jab of fear surge through her spine. Just as she'd always loved dolphins, she'd always been terrified of sharks.

'Where?'

'They chase dolphins, see.'

And Amazon realized that she'd been wrong about the dark shapes under the water. Now she could see that they moved in a completely different way to the dolphins – a sinuous, snake-like back-and-forth motion, rather than the up and down of the sea mammals. And the tips of their vertical tails cut the surface of the lagoon in a way that the horizontal tails of the dolphins never did.

Amazon didn't need another invitation, and in a few seconds she and Frazer were climbing into the narrow canoe. The two village children were standing, the boy at the front and the girl at the back, but Amazon and Frazer knelt in between them, and held on tight to the wooden sides. There was hardly enough room for the four of them: this wasn't one of the big, ocean-going canoes the men of the village used for fishing expeditions out beyond the reef, but a frail and fragile craft designed to be used in the shelter of the lagoon. It had a small sail made from woven palm fronds on a bamboo frame, but it was useless without the wind, and was lying flat in the bottom of the vessel, which is why the two village children had used the bamboo poles to push the craft along.

Amazon found that she was trembling. 'Are we safe here?' she asked.

'I guess so. The sharks don't seem very interested in us – they just want that calf.' Then Frazer turned to their rescuers. 'Thanks, you guys. I'm Frazer Hunt, and this is my cousin, Amazon.'

'I am Oti,' said the boy. 'This is sister. She called Mahina. You pretty stupid to swim with sharks.'

'If we'd known there were sharks . . .' began Amazon, but then she remembered the dolphins. 'There must be something we could do to help them?'

Frazer thought for a moment. 'I wonder what's stopping them from going back out through the gap in the reef . . .'

'Sharks don't let,' said Oti. 'See, more of them swim in front of it.'

What had been a confused picture was becoming clearer to Amazon. The mother and baby would make sudden darting runs towards the gap, but the sharks would not let them pass. The mother would butt at any that came too close to her calf, but she could not force a way through to the open ocean, and safety.

'Can you get the canoe over there, Oti? Maybe the sharks will clear off if we sit over the gap.'

The Polynesian boy looked doubtful. 'This is not wise. There is some danger.'

'Oh, please,' Amazon implored. 'I couldn't bear it if that little dolphin . . .'

Oti shrugged. 'OK. We try.'

There was still no wind for the canoe's small sail, so Oti and Mahina used the bamboo poles to punt the canoe along.

When they reached the gap, the sharks, far from being scared off, seemed to become more excited and gathered around this new intruder, giving Amazon her first good look at them. Some were just a little longer than her outstretched arms; others were a couple of metres from tail to nose.

Amazon shuddered. She knew that it was silly to regard any animal as evil: she understood perfectly well that all creatures were engaged in the same struggle to survive, to get enough to eat and to reproduce. But there was just something unfathomably wicked about the sharp, pointed noses, the staring eyes with their black, slit-like pupils, the mouth, half hidden, but full of pitiless teeth.

'We're lucky,' said Frazer. 'These are just reef sharks, by the look of them.'

'So they don't eat people, then?'

'Nah. They might bite your foot off if you dangled it in front of them, but that's about it.'

'I'd quite like to keep my feet, actually,' said Amazon, pulling her toes in from the edge of the canoe.

'If there was a tiger shark here,' Frazer continued, 'things would be a lot less pleasant. Hey, I've had an idea. Maybe we can use the poles to drive them away from the gap, so the dolphins can escape. What do you say, Oti?'

'Can try,' said the Polynesian boy, without much confidence. 'But we must have care. Small canoe not good out in big sea.'

The gap in the coral was about four metres wide. Beyond the shelter of the reef the water was choppier and, now that the canoe was in the gap, it rose and fell with the waves.

Mahina gave Frazer her pole, and he and Oti jabbed them down at the sharks. It was almost impossible to hit the creatures. The sharks slipped elegantly aside from the thrusts. Oti was used to spear fishing from the canoe, and easily kept his balance, but Frazer had more trouble. Once he jabbed his pole with such force that he almost fell in amongst the angry sharks. He instinctively grabbed hold of Amazon, and would have dragged her into the water with him if it had not been for the quickness and agility of little Mahina, who steadied them both.

However, despite their difficulties, they had some success in at least irritating the sharks enough for them to move away.

'Come on now!' Amazon cried out to the dolphins, who had been keeping well clear of the action. 'Time to make a run for it.'

The dolphin mother seemed to be paying attention. When the last of the bigger sharks swam away, she made another of her rushes for the open sea, followed closely by the calf.

And this time it looked like they were going to make it. The sharks realized what was happening and raced back to try to catch the dolphins before they escaped, but they were too late. In a straight race, the mammals were much too quick. They were halfway through the reef opening, and Amazon had already begun to cheer.

But then something huge and ominous loomed from the seaward side of the reef. This was no foot-chewing shark. It was longer than the canoe, and dwarfed the mother dolphin.

Frazer recognized it immediately. It was a tiger shark, the most feared killer in these seas. Too big to risk swimming into the lagoon at low tide, it had, with the ancient cunning of its kind, been waiting patiently outside.

And now its time had come.

It was certainly powerful enough to tackle a fully grown bottle-nosed dolphin, but very few hunters will take the parent when the helpless child is up for grabs. And so the shark lunged with deadly intent towards the calf, its wide mouth gaping obscenely.

Superb swimmer though she was, the mother was moving too quickly to turn in time to protect her infant. Trapped between the wall of the reef and the jaws of the predator, the calf had nowhere left to swim. Or so Amazon thought, and her joyful shout turned into a cry of horror.

But a couple of strong beats from its tail sent the calf up and out of the water. The tiger shark's jaws closed on nothing but the surging wake.

Amazon and Frazer gasped together as the dolphin flew through the air, and landed with a splash in the shallow water – no more than a hand's width – washing over the reef itself. It flapped and flopped, but the sharp coral cut into its delicate skin, and soon it lay still.

The shark sensed that its victim was close. It tried to surge up on to the reef, the alternating light and dark stripes on its enormous back rippling in the light. But the calf was too far away, and the shark couldn't reach it. For a moment it seemed that the predator would be stranded on top of the reef as well. But the shark managed to thrash itself down from the coral, and rolled away, beating its long tail.

The calf was making a desperate bleating noise, calling out hopelessly to its mother. The mother dolphin circled round, and made her own clicks and clacks in response. But she could not come too close as the tiger was back on patrol, seeking revenge.

The canoe had come to rest right up against the reef. The dolphin calf was tantalizingly close, but out of reach. Amazon could not stand its plaintive calling. She had to do something, but she knew that if she tried to walk on the reef her feet would be cut to shreds on the sharp coral.

'I'm saving that dolphin,' she said, and before the others could stop her she picked up the useless sail from the bottom of the canoe, and threw it on top of the reef. Then – accompanied by a cry of dismay from Frazer – she stepped from the flimsy canoe on to the sail. She felt her feet sink through the woven palm leaves and press on the coral, but the sail gave her just enough protection. In three quick steps she had reached the little calf.

It was so beautiful, so helpless. She knelt by its side and put her hand on its nose. It looked back at her, and seemed calmed, as if it knew that she meant it only well. Amazon would happily have spent an hour there, just gazing at this wondrous creature, but she knew that she had to work fast. Already the dolphin's skin was cut and torn, and she could almost feel the agony of the hot sun on its back. She worked her hands and then arms under its body, and lifted it up from the reef. It was heavier than she'd imagined, and she almost slipped and fell.

But Amazon was strong and, even more than that, determined. Staggering under the weight, she made it to the edge of the reef. The mother came in close, followed not far behind by the tiger shark. It was now or never. Amazon dropped the baby into the sea, just clear of the reef, hoping it would know to swim away with all its might.

But the calf was still dazed and confused, and it hesitated for a fatal few seconds. The tiger was on it again. But this time the mother was ready. She propelled herself like a torpedo at the shark, ramming it with a crunching force that propelled the giant fish sideways against the reef.

And then mother and calf were away, flying joyfully though the gentle waves, and no shark was ever going to catch them.

'Take that, you overgrown anchovy,' yelled Amazon, pumping her fist in the air.

It was a mistake.

The woven leaves that made up the sail were slippery and coming apart in the thin layer of water that washed over the coral. Amazon stumbled backwards, half righted herself and then over-compensated, falling headlong into the sea, outside the reef, just metres from the waiting tiger shark.